T0368084

THE REFLEX

PART 2
2ND BOOK IN THE REFLEX SERIES

MARIA DENISON

BALBOA.PRESS
A DIVISION OF HAY HOUSE

Balboa Press books may be ordered through booksellers or by contacting:

Balboa Press
A Division of Hay House
1663 Liberty Drive
Bloomington, IN 47403
www.balboapress.com
844-682-1282

Because of the dynamic nature of the Internet, any web addresses or links contained in this book may have changed since publication and may no longer be valid. The views expressed in this work are solely those of the author and do not necessarily reflect the views of the publisher, and the publisher hereby disclaims any responsibility for them.

The author of this book does not dispense medical advice or prescribe the use of any technique as a form of treatment for physical, emotional, or medical problems without the advice of a physician, either directly or indirectly. The intent of the author is only to offer information of a general nature to help you in your quest for emotional and spiritual well-being. In the event you use any of the information in this book for yourself, which is your constitutional right, the author and the publisher assume no responsibility for your actions.

Any people depicted in stock imagery provided by Getty Images are models, and such images are being used for illustrative purposes only.
Certain stock imagery © Getty Images.

Cover Design by: Claudia Kemmerer Design

Print information available on the last page.

ISBN: 979-8-7652-3859-2 (sc)
ISBN: 979-8-7652-3861-5 (hc)
ISBN: 979-8-7652-3860-8 (e)

Library of Congress Control Number: 2022908086

Balboa Press rev. date: 02/21/2023

CONTENTS

PROLOGUE

(Recap of the last pages of Part 1. If you need a reminder, please read. If you just want to skim or skip, please do, and proceed to Chapter 1)

AS THE TEENAGERS ARRIVE, EVERYONE gets seated in the living room, but Reed is still standing. Cara runs to her favorite chair to take a seat but can't get comfortable. She stands back up and looks at the cushion. Feeling it with her hands, she doesn't locate any issues. She sits back down but is still bothered. Rising once again, she pulls the cushion off to look underneath it. Her suspicion is one of the kids hid some contraband below. It's clean, though. She repositions the cushion but does not sit. Instead, she stands stiffly looking at the chair.

Her discomfort is not the lovely, upholstered armchair. The tension in the room is substantial. Something is wrong. Cara is scrutinizing in all directions. *There's a threat. I know it. It's that prickles on the neck thing happening.* Slowly looking around her, she rests her gaze out the wall of windows facing the backyard. It's not out there. The tension and threat to do harm is in the room with her.

Cara turns to her children who are seated on the couch with their backs to the glass wall. Sitting with Eli, all of them appear bored. She shifts her eyes to Jinx and Jake. Jinx is reprimanding her husband to use a coaster on Cara's side table for his coffee. Nic and Sasha are seated in the two leather club chairs across from them in deep discussion. No one is paying any attention to her or noticing the problem.

Her scrutiny finally rests on Reed. He's still standing, and right next to her, his eyes locked on her. Cara peers into those eyes and sees imminent peril reflected back at her. The threat is emanating from him. Her head tilts in confusion. Reed has his ice face on, and it's directed right at her. She is dumbfounded. Reed has directed mad, raging, frustrated and betrayed faces at her, but she has never seen him look at her like this. He's wearing his ready to kill you face. Without breaking eye contact with her, Reed slowly reaches inside his jacket.

Suddenly, Cara lunges towards him, grabbing his wrist with both her hands. "Stop."

"Stop what?" Reed asks quietly.

She backs away slightly, but then he gets his hand further into his jacket. She firms her grip on his wrist. "NO, STOP!"

Nic sees the confrontation and gets up to head towards her and Reed, but Sasha jumps out in front of him preventing his progress.

Still locked in a battle over his wrist, Reed calmly inquires, "C, what's the matter," but his face and glaring eyes are cruel. His pale baby blue eyes have turned frigid.

Staring intently into those glaciers with bewilderment and determination, Cara states firmly, "I need you to take your hand out of your jacket, NOW!"

Reed, still with that forbidding glare, "But I'm just getting my phone, C."

She shakes her head, but nothing changes the threat she's feeling from Reed. "You're lying. Your phone is not in your jacket."

"C, let go of my wrist, now, before I have to hurt you."

Nic tries to push past Sasha, but Sasha grabs him hard, and Nic's confusion prevents him from fighting back.

Cara is completely panicked. This is all wrong. Reed wants to hurt her. She's sure of it. "No, you ARE trying to hurt me. Why do you want to hurt me? TELL ME!"

Reed grabs Cara so quickly, she doesn't see it coming. He has restrained both of her arms and is shaking her. Nic is flipping his head back and forth between the confrontation and Sasha. Sasha only takes a firmer hold on him.

Cara is close to hysterics. Reed is in her face now, those awful eyes on her. *I feel his hatred. I don't understand. He loves me.*

Reed yells into her face, "TELL ME WHAT'S IN MY JACKET IF IT'S NOT MY PHONE! TELL ME!"

"YOU HAVE A GUN!"

Reed shakes her harder, "OF COURSE I HAVE A GUN HOLSTERED IN THERE!"

A sudden jolt of pain spears through her brain. It's dizzying, but she can see a clear picture of what he has. "No, no, not that gun!" Cara pleadingly whispers back at him.

"WHAT DO I HAVE IN HERE, CARA," Reed demands.

Cara blurts out, unchecked and uncensored, from somewhere unfamiliar, "You have Sasha's gun!"

With Cara's declaration, Reed releases his firm hold but gently runs his hands down her arms, massaging where he had gripped her. Sasha releases Nic and all eyes are on Cara and him. Reed opens his jacket and deliberately pulls out a vintage Makarov PM pistol. He walks towards Sasha and hands it to him. Nic is staring at the gun with recognition because it is from Sasha's collection. He looks up at Cara, tilting his head.

Cara is standing by herself, trembling, one hand on her forehead. Her eyes shift to Nic, who's frozen in place. Reed slowly approaches to stand in front of her. His heart bursts with love and sympathy for her. "I am so sorry, my sweetheart, but it had to be done. We couldn't figure out a better way to make it happen. And we can't move forward anymore without knowing for sure," Reed says as gently as possible. Cara looks up at him with tears in her eyes, unable to speak.

Nic tries to finally move, and finds Sasha stepping out in front of him, again. He places a hand on Nic's shoulder, "Nicolae, please, we must see this through. Trust me," Sasha says soothingly.

Reed can only gaze at Cara. "C, sweetheart, this is my fault. I was your handler, and I was so remiss. I just didn't see it. It was all right in front of me, and I didn't put it together. Maybe, I didn't want to see it. Again, I am so sorry," he tells her with all the guilt and resignation he feels.

Cara questions him with a shaky voice, "What did I just do?"

Stroking her hair, he admits, "You did what you've been able to do since I met you, sweetheart. It's been there all this time."

Cara always knew what to do. She could always predict everyone's next move. She was amazing in the field, yet she couldn't get through a simulation. Reed thought she was a natural, but her intuition was too sharp. He should have seen it but chose not to. When he looks back, he thinks himself a fool. And then everything clicked into place on the plane ride back from Berlin. He had a moment of illumination.

When she started singing the song Nic was humming. It was then. The illumination was blinding. She kept asking if he remembered about Nic's humming, and of course he had, but Nic wasn't humming. He was sitting right next to Nic, and Cara was across the table, at least four more feet away. And he knows for a fact her hearing is not as keen as his.

"You didn't hear Nic humming, C; you heard the music in his head." Cara is backing away from him, shakily, tears running down her face. "You hear a lot of stuff in everyone's head, C. I predict you feel what's in their hearts, as well." He is almost pedantic in his delivery. "You're not a natural, my dangerous, little sweetheart. You're a bit of a cheater."

With this accusation, Nic tries to get past Sasha, but again, he restrains him. Cara is only focused on Reed as he continues his slow revelation.

It all reconciles when Reed thinks back to Kabul. Why was Kabul a failure? Why didn't Cara feel or 'hear' those men coming into the alley with her? There were six of them. Something went wrong in her sonar. Then, there's Geneva; she was a mess. First time Reed had ever seen it. "You were so fucked up and out of sorts in Geneva, it spilled over to me," he confesses.

But the pinnacle was yesterday morning. Reed listened to the tapes of her conversation with Vlad. She was doing great. She had him talking, and giving up information, and then suddenly, she shut down. Training gone. Sonar gone. Cara jammed. She went off to seizure land. "What do those three occurrences, the only times you fell apart on a mission, have as a common denominator, C?"

Cara's gaze shifts to take in her husband. Nic brings his eyes to hers, but his face reveals nothing.

Reed continues his assertions. "I berated you over Nic, your fascination, your obsession, your complete failure to see any reason whatsoever. You have NEVER been that way. What made Nic different? True Love? That's for Hollywood and romance novels. No one gets that from just seeing one another across a dusty Afghani alley."

At this statement, Jinx and Jake rise from their seats. Jinx can't stop herself; she interrupts Reed's monologue. "It's not normal what you and Nic have, Cara. It isn't. I'm sorry but Reed's right. You two are something else, sometimes. Like too in sync. Unnatural for a couple. And the chemistry still? After 17 years together?"

Reed needed to confirm his suspicion. Cara is not what she appears. She is more than that. The clues were everywhere but he didn't bother to recognize them. "Somehow, your brain isn't processing it, but you're reading people's minds. And you're not alone," he delivers with intensity, wanting effect.

Reed starts to back away from Cara as she begins to sway. *Can this even be true?!* She sees movement to her right and notices Jake coming closer to her. She turns her head to glance at him and…*He's so scary. Why does he always have that awful menacing look?*

That's the only look he has. In her mind, it's as clear as if Nic had spoken out loud.

She spins her head to Nic so hard it causes her to become unbalanced. *Nic? Baby?*

Cara goes down, knees crumpling beneath her at the sound of her husband's voice in her mind. Jake manages to catch her before she hits the ground. Nic's still unmoving, staring wild-eyed at her. He's as shocked by what's happened as she.

Cara mia!

I'm okay, I'm okay. She sends that thought out to him with some strength.

WHAT THE HELL IS HAPPENING? Not only can she hear him, but also feel his fear and confusion. Nic reaches her and scoops her out of Jake's arms, falling to his knees. The children are horrified. The entire room is frozen in place, everyone gawking at her and Nic.

Nic turns angrily to Sasha and Reed, "This is what you two talked about last night, isn't it!?"

CHAPTER 1

CARA'S THROBBING HEAD HAS BECOME more of a dull ache. Her body is still trembling as she not only hears her husband's thoughts for the first time ever, but also feels his rage. All of it directed at Reed and Sasha. With one arm wrapped around her and his other arm out, finger pointed at both, Nic screams, "This what you two talked about last night, isn't it!?"

Sasha doesn't look apologetic when he answers. "It was all there, Nic. Reed is correct. I am to blame as well. You...you are different. I grew to love you like a brother, so I didn't want to see it. But it was there. You are like Cara, somehow. You are you, but more. It explains so much I've taken for granted over the years."

While Sasha is talking, Reed approaches and leans into her, placing his lips to her ear. She flinches, but he holds her head, firmly. "Tell Jinx it's time to start drinking, and to get some alcohol out here...with your mind." He backs away, but his eyes are fixed on her in silent command.

She places her hand on Nic's face and gazes into his eyes before Jinx jumps up and announces, "Shit, I don't know about you guys, but I need to start drinking. Do I have any takers?"

Cara inhales so hard, her heart literally skips a beat. She's not even sure how she did that. Reed answers Jinx, calmly requesting she open a bottle of red, but his eyes remain on Cara.

Sasha adds, "Jinx, do you mind going down to the wine cellar and getting the Russian River Pinot, please? You know I love that one." He smiles at his joke.

Oblivious, Jinx heads out to descend the stairs. When she is out of earshot, Reed commands, "C, tell her to grab the Frascati for something lighter, as well." Jake moves towards Reed when he realizes the game they're playing with Jinx. Reed puts up his hand to stop him from overreacting. "I'm sorry, it must be done. Please let this play out."

Three minutes go by while no one speaks or appears to breathe. All eyes are darting around the room, looking from one to the other. Jinx starts talking as soon as she's at the top of the stairs. "You know, I grabbed a bottle of Frascati, too. It's nice and light for anyone not looking for the heavy Pinot this early." There's a collective gasp heard around the room.

Jake reaches for his wife and gently pulls her into the living room, taking the two bottles from her. "What happened?" Jinx inquires seeing the shocked look on all their faces.

"When the mission script had to change, how did you know where C needed you to be in the field, Jinx?" Reed demands.

Jinx is confused by his inquisition. "Most times I guessed based on what she would do."

"But you always guessed correctly, didn't you?"

"Well, sure?" Jake takes Jinx's hand and tells her discreetly what just occurred. "WHAT?" Turning and glaring at Cara, she yells, "You've been manipulating me?!"

Reed, again, takes control, "Jinx, calm down. I don't believe C does it consciously. When she NEEDS you, it projects to you."

Cara and Nic are still on the ground speechless, both feeling anxious and perplexed. Cara's head is starting to clear, though. *Nic, it's all true, isn't it?*

It would appear that way, cara mia.

Do I manipulate you?

No.

How can you be so sure? I mean, I manipulate people all the time. It's common knowledge, but I didn't realize I had mad skills at it.

I'm not sure how, but I do know, and you don't have that effect on me. I think Reed has a direction he's going with this. Can you read anyone else's thoughts like you're reading mine right now?

She scans the room. *I'm getting a sense of some thoughts from Sasha, Reed, and Jinx. None are clear like yours and mine, though. Jake is closed off completely. So are all three kids.*

Interesting. He muses.

Are you processing with that brilliant brain of yours?

Yes.

Why can't I hear or see that, the processing? Just your words. I imagine you're speaking in your head like I am.

I am speaking them, but I don't know why you can't see more.

Cara deflates. She takes in a big breath to reorient her body. *Nic, did my cliché B grade movie life just become science fiction?*

She can hear him sigh in her mind. *Which answer do you want, cara mia? The one that makes you feel better, or the one my brain is processing right now?*

Before she can mentally respond to Nic, Jake comes to their side on the floor. "You're talking to each right now, telepathically?" Jake inquires, kindly, considerate of their feelings.

"Yes," Nic states.

"So, you can hear her thoughts like Jinx can, but you can also project your thoughts to her?" Jake questions, directing his inquiry only to Nic.

"Yes."

"You have never done this consciously before?"

"No, we have not."

"But you have had a connection to one another that's deeper and more intimate than most couples." This genteel Jake is foreign to Cara. Nic nods his answer and Jake continues, "It never occurred to you to explore that, or think it 'odd'?"

"No." Nic hesitates for a moment. "Maybe?"

Jake very calmly sits back on the floor with his legs spread to each side of Cara and Nic. He leans into the couch behind him, getting comfortable, before turning hard and casting a menacing glare towards Sasha and Reed.

Pointing his finger between the two of them, he accuses, "You two little co-conspirators have no idea what you've just done." He points to her and Nic, who are obviously in distress, before addressing Sasha and Reed again. "Subtlety is neither one of your talents, is it?"

Reed suddenly looks very guilty as his eyes move to Cara's tear-stained face. He immediately babbles on about how he did some quick research on the plane and read how their gift could be pushed into the conscious level with an emotional breakthrough. He admits he spoke to Sasha about the situation last night, and they couldn't think of a better way to make that happen than to trick Cara.

Sasha jumps in and apologizes but adds they were both tired and knew they didn't have much time to come up with a plan.

"You are both dumbasses," Jake reprimands. "Did it not occur to you that this emotional scene could have been avoided by just discussing it with them?" Jake continues to chastise Reed and Sasha. "Breakthroughs can occur many different ways. Sending someone over the edge is only one means. You came at this ill-equipped and unprepared. Although you achieved the required result, you could have accomplished it with a kinder, gentler hand."

● ● ●

Placing one hand on Nic's leg and one on Cara's, Jake decides he needs to elaborate for all of them to contain the hysteria he feels building in the room. "What just happened isn't magic or fiction, it's only science. What I'm about to tell you may be hard to take, and may blow your minds a little bit, but hear me out.

"Many great physicists, including Einstein, have envisaged the existence of the particular anomaly you've just seen displayed, and Nic and Cara are, by far, not the first to have this gift. It's all about the ability to convert thoughts into energy. Our thoughts have a molecular structure like everything else in the world. Those molecular particles have energy. Some people can manipulate that energy with their minds the way your brain tells you to lift an arm when you want to reach for something. It's the same concept."

Research and experiments in this field of science have been going on for decades. The physics portion aside, it begins with the notion of intuition. Why do some people have more acute intuition than others? Some minds process information on an intuitive level first, while other minds can only process information given the facts. Many personality tests, like the Myers Briggs, for instance, have been around for decades and are used to determine which type of mind one possesses. These tests are often utilized to gauge someone's career choice, learning challenges, even which type of mate is most suitable.

Other researchers began to look more closely at the concept of intuition. What occurs organically in the brain to cause it to view the world from an intuitive level? That research has led to a more biological understanding of neuropathways in the mind, and how information is moved on the synapses firing on those pathways. It's sometimes referred to as neuroplasticity, the ability to alter and change the neurons and synapses in the brain. Much of this research has led to breakthroughs on ways to approach and treat traumatic brain injuries, how to help Parkinson's victims, and aided in mental illness solutions and drug therapies. But what is ultimately known of the human brain is still a very fractional understanding.

Still other doctors and researchers have moved toward the concept that our brains are only functioning at ten percent of their capacity. Those scientists have been more inclined to believe intuition is the result of a special talent. A gift. They believe the mind can acquire the ability to utilize and manipulate those neuropathways to produce an evolved outcome. "Tons of research has been funded in this direction, although some of it may be questionable in its ethics. Regardless, there have been some documented results of psychic gifts." Jakes looks around the room to find all eyes directly on him.

"Here's where some of the confusion and perhaps skepticism presents itself." Jake continues with his lecture. "Despite your brain's capacity to possibly produce a 'gifted' moment, between the biology, the psychology, and the physics associated with the event, everyone's mind has some conflict with it."

First off, the concept of the 'breakthrough' is highly debated. Psychologically, every mind is broken into levels of consciousness and sub consciousness. Consciousness is the editor of the mind. It inherently filters inconsistencies for the mind. Any input it's getting from the subconscious, or any input it receives from the reality around it, will be discarded if it makes no cerebral sense. Normal, sane brains function this way.

Jake points to Cara and uses her as an example. "Cara may have been hearing people's thoughts at an early age. Her subconscious released that chatter to her conscious, but it rejected it. It may have rejected it because it was incongruent. It made no sense. Or it may have rejected it because all the chatter was too overwhelming to process. Either way, her subconscious has been protecting her, keeping the chatter to a minimum. So, the information is there, but she is accessing it only on an instinctive level."

Pointing to Nic to make his next example, Jake expands, "Nic's brain may have been receiving the input but, biologically, the neuropathways didn't exist yet, to allow the chatter to make the clear jump from subconscious to conscious. So, again, the information is there, but it has no means to move because the synapses to reach its destination don't exist. Neuropathways can be created and repaired in the brain. Doctors have discovered this by monitoring the progress of healing from brain injuries. A breakthrough can be that path suddenly developing."

Jake adds, "The physics portion of this, well, that's complicated and confusing."

Physics theories would argue both Cara and Nic were born with these abilities; their brains were engineered with the ability to manipulate energy on an evolved level. The details on how they are doing it is the complicated and confusing part. And none of those details are factual at this point. It's all theories and equational math. "String theory, quantum mechanics and the God particle are all still only theories to suggest we are one with our universe," Jake says, glancing at the three teenagers on the couch. "Are you still with me?" he asks with a wink.

Nic has been listening to Jake intently. He's looking much more composed as he pulls Cara tighter to him and runs his fingers through her hair. Nic lets his gaze travel around the great room before resting on Jake. "Thank you, Jake, for your assistance. Apparently, our handlers are a bit inept when it comes to 'handling' a situation. A simple game of guess what number I'm thinking in my head may have sufficed, don't you think?" He glares at Sasha and Reed before turning his attention back to Jake. "But, how is it you know so much about this?"

A shot of panic runs up Jake's spine. He has offered too much. He shakes his head sadly at Nic and resignedly asks, "Ever hear of the Stargate Project?"

CHAPTER 2

NIC COCKS HIS HEAD AT Jake, but Cara releases the death grip she has on her husband to gawk at Reed in puzzlement.

Reed's mouth has dropped open as he studies Jake. He may know who Jake is, but his knowledge of the Stargate project? This is new intel. The mysterious Jake is starting to make more sense. He finally gets his mouth to work. "Were you a part of that program?"

Nodding solemnly, Jake admits he was placed into the program initially, when he was 13 years old. Nothing came of it, but he learned much about what they were trying to accomplish. He was admitted back in for more tests before he left for college. After that, involvement became voluntary, and he chose not to be a part of it. When he did run into people who were still in the program, he would get updates, but never offered to come back in.

Reed catches on before realizing not everyone else knows what Jake's talking about. Mostly addressing the kids, he explains, "The Stargate Project was the overall code name for a cumulative directive during the Cold War to find and test individuals for psychic, or what they referred to as RV, or Remote Viewing, capabilities. RV was the term used for decades to describe the ability to project one's mind to a particular location. Nowadays it's also referred to as astral projection. During the Cold War, the superpowers decided research into RV had some merit. The research was funded with the hopes of locating, or producing soldiers, who could project their minds over an area to gain intel, the concept being one could 'spy' intel by remotely viewing it."

Sasha adds, "Both the USSR and China had similar programs."

Reed continues, "There have been some stories circulated of small successes during the 70's and 80's, but the understanding was both the Russian and US programs were abandoned in the 1990's. In the US, the talk was the program didn't have adequate success, and with the advent of technology, intel-gathering has been allocated to satellites, high tech listening devices, and most recently drones."

Mia interrupts Reed. "So, you're saying governments were spending considerable time and money trying to find people and test them to see if they could RV, and like read minds, to get information for military purposes? But then just scrapped it when they saw their efforts weren't producing their army of mind readers, and realizing technology could adequately replace the need?"

"That was the word on the street, so to speak. Remember, these programs were originally developed well before computers, let alone stealth planes and bugging devices," Reed confirms, but adds, "While your mom, Jinx and I were at Langley, it was circulated the program just couldn't be justified, and the money better spent on technology.

"The Stargate Project originated within the CIA by taking much of the private research being done at Institutes and Universities and bringing it in house. In the late 70's, the CIA transferred the project to the Defense Intelligence Agency. Offices were established at Fort Meade Army Base, and the research continued there until 1995 when the project, and all its files and data, were transferred back to the CIA for evaluation. A panel at the CIA determined the Stargate Project hadn't produced significant results, and the project, and any funding for it, was shut down," Reed concludes.

"So, that's how I know so much about this," Jake sadly offers when Reed is finished with his explanation. However, before Reed can ask him more questions, Jake changes direction with, "Because of that, I would like to try something with Nic and Cara."

Curious as to what Jake has in mind, Reed moves closer to the three of them on the floor. Sasha is right behind him, also anxious to listen to the conversation.

"Cara, can you see past what Nic is projecting?" Jake inquires, kindly.

"No, we were talking about it. I can hear his voice…but can't hear or see anything else," Cara explains with a shaky voice that Reed is feeling guilty about. He wants to wrap her in his arms, but now isn't the time.

Jake continues with patience and surprising calm. "I'm going to hold your hand. I'll explain why later but will you take my hand?" Cara reaches out to him and clasps his hand.

Jake wants Nic to mentally rapid-fire random numbers out to Cara. But before he does that, he wants Cara to close her eyes and search her mind to see if she can pinpoint where they are appearing. "If you can locate them, you're going to…people describe it differently…but…build a bridge, create a path, form a tunnel, follow a thread." Cara jerks at his last choice of word. "Can you follow a thread?" She nods. "Good, let's try this. Nic, start."

Cara shuts her eyes and can see where the numbers are, and the thick thread-like pull string they are attached to. *I see them, Nic! I'm going to pull the thread.*

Suddenly, Cara's eyes go wide, and her breathing becomes shallow and fast. Nic has grabbed her shoulders at the same time.

"Cara, can you say out loud what you see, please?" Jake requests, again, using a soothing voice.

She raises her head to the ceiling, and her eyes are open, but she only has the visual of what's in her mind. She gets to her knees while Nic is still holding her shoulders. She struggles to verbalize what she sees. All she can do is stare blankly at the sight above her. "Nic, what is this? It's amazing."

"It's my grid," Nic answers matter-of-factly.

She is gazing at the ceiling, eyes darting from section to section, her face displaying complete awe at what she's seeing. It's like looking at a massive computer screen with over twenty separate search windows open for viewing. "You see this all the time in your mind?"

"Yes, it's how I work the different sections of my brain. How I do the math and calculations. Do you see the bottom right quadrant? That's the math area. See, it's running numbers now. It's always calculating."

"What's the upper left doing?"

"It's scanning the area around us, kind of like a GPS. It's plotting each item and where it is, its mass, volume, density, distance, etcetera." Nic seems unfazed by this.

Cara is still looking up. She's squinting without realizing it, trying vainly to focus with her eyes. She just now found the quadrant with all the music. She smiles wide. "It's like a massive iTunes account. Your song lists have associated sheet music attached. It's your running Soundtrack. It's always on in the background, the music, isn't it?"

"It runs at different volumes, but it's always playing," Nic offers.

Cara's head falls to meet her husband's eyes with horror. "You do realize this isn't, um, typical or normal?"

"You don't have a grid?"

"Babe, if I had that in my head 24/7, I would be institutionalized." She points to the ceiling. "This is intense. How do you stay sane?"

"I can turn it down, watch."

And suddenly the multi-windowed screen loses most of its illumination. "Ohhhh, it's like you dimmed the lights. Does it turn off completely?"

"No, but I can 'dim' it down quite a bit," Nic answers with a chuckle.

"So, you've always had this…grid, and you've learned to live with it?"

"I guess." At this, Nic turns to look at Sasha. "Do you have a grid?" Sasha shakes his head. "How do you do the math thing in your head?" Sasha only shrugs.

Cara surmised early in her relationship with Nic that he possessed a photographic memory. He could also solve complicated math equations in his mind. Since she has known Sasha, he's displayed the same talents. Come to think of it, so has Jake.

This brutally organized mind screen is nothing she could ever imagine. If she forgets her shopping list, she can barely recall half of it at the grocery store. A grid would be handy, but she could never look at that in her mind all the time.

Cara looks back to Jake to ask if he has a crazy grid, but he's smiling proudly at her with his thumb rubbing the top of her hand. She smiles back at him, unsure why he appears so pleased.

"Little darling, do you realize what you just did?" Jake asks her.

Cara slowly lets out, "I visited Nic's mind?"

Jake laughs before pulling her into a hug. "Visited is one way to put it."

Getting a hug from Jake is usually reserved for celebrations. She's not sure why he's so thrilled. He must sense her hesitation because he pulls her from his chest. Looking only into her eyes, he explains, "What you just did was take a portion of your consciousness and bring it with you as you traveled over Nic's thread. Essentially, passing a piece of you to Nic." He studies her before adding, "I have only heard of the possibility of doing this but have never known anyone to have success with it."

As he continues to peer only at her, Cara 'receives' an image, like a snapshot of Jake's thoughts. She blurts, "You're wondering if I have successfully made the jump and cleared a path between my sub and waking mind or established a few new neuropathways." He gives her a big smile in acknowledgment, so she adds, "You have an eidetic mind." He nods to her in affirmation. "Do you have a grid like Nic?"

Jake cants his head. "Not that I am aware of, but can you look in there and see if I do, little darling?"

Smiling at his endearment, Cara shakes her head. Jake has been referring to her as 'little darling' for years. It's odd because at 5' 6" and almost 140 pounds, she is built like a brick shithouse. But compared to every single person in this room, she is the smallest. It's nice to feel petite in a crowd. That's a rarity, when by today's standards, she is considered a beast if she can't fit her ass into size 2 pants.

The movement is subtle, but her husband's hands tug her bottom, easily drawing her onto his lap. His arm wraps tightly just under her breasts. His lips to her ear, he blows out a breath, but his words are for her mind only. *Don't ever put yourself down. This body could always stop traffic and still does.* All she can do is place a hand over his and promise to watch her self-castigation in the future; now that her mind is apparently a public space.

Turning back to Jake and his question, she refocuses. "I tried earlier. I tried to scan everyone in the room, but I only get fleeting glimpses, more feelings than thoughts. You were completely closed off, until just now, when I 'received' a peek."

Wrapping his huge hands around her biceps, Jake positions her off Nic so she is kneeling between his spread legs. It's the most intimate she's ever been with Jake. For the first time since she's been speaking with him, she glances to her right at Sasha and Reed. They are kneeling right behind Nic and watching raptly. "That's because I'm blocking you," Jake says drawing Cara's eyes back to him.

Then she receives another peek at his thoughts. Jake suspects everyone in the room is blocking her without realizing it. He's certain that's why they are all friends. It's not as Reed has inferred. Rather, she and Nic are special because they found each other. Yes, their gifts complement one another, but so too do Reed and the others. To some extent, they all must possess some gifts. If Cara and Nic were around people with no special gift, they would be constantly bombarded with those thoughts. It would have been too overwhelming.

Understanding Jake's explanation, Cara cries out, "My seizures! I was getting too much input from the outside world."

Realizing she once again read his thoughts, Jake smiles at her and asks, "What about growing up with your family? Do you recall if your seizures came as often, or starting early in your childhood?"

She must think about this answer. They are her family, so they irritate her sometimes. It's not the same as feeling overwhelmed or bombarded. From her own experience, she knows dealing with one's family elicits a generally accepted level of distress for everyone. She can't recall having any of her meltdowns or fugue states with them, though. She finally answers simply, "No."

Jake chuckles at her hesitation, almost as if he heard *her* thoughts. But he becomes serious once again, directing, "I'm going to let you inside my head, but you need to promise to only look where I let you, okay?" She nods, understanding he is a man with secrets, and this is a big step for him. He moves those huge hands down from her biceps until he's threading his fingers into hers. "I'm going to reach out to you, now. Find the thread."

Closing her eyes to block out everyone, she focuses only in her mind. What she visualizes, as a result, can only be described as amazing. She can see that thread to Jake, but she can see many other thicker threads, as well. Only her side of them is visible, but it's extraordinary. She's momentarily lost in the landscape before she remembers what the objective was. She concentrates on Jake's thread and attempts to travel along like she did with Nic. She's struggling, though. It feels like walking through a murky fog, slow and dark. It's nothing like the experience just now with Nic.

Trying to walk the group through her experiences, she narrates, "I see images. But they're not clear like with Nic. Wait, I see your grid! It's not like Nic's…it's…less complicated but there's a resemblance. Everything is opaque, though." Cara is trying to see in the fog but isn't getting anything to come into clear focus. "Jake, may I try something?"

Before he can answer, Jake inhales and shudders. "What did you do?"

"I tried to send you a picture of Nic's grid," Cara responds, alarmed that she's hurt him.

"Holy shit! I see it crystal clear. I just didn't know what the hell it was!" Jake jerks his head to Nic. "THIS is in your mind?" Nic nods. "It's fucking fantastic! Okay, we need to try something else now that I've seen this." Cara has never seen Jake so animated.

Jake asks Nic, "Can you see on your grid where Cara is coming through?" Nic confirms he can. Jake wants him to go to Cara the way she came to him. Follow the thread to her, and travel over it. Jake releases Cara's hands and places them into Nic's. "The physical contact is like support. I'll explain later what else it does. Go ahead and try it."

Ready, baby?

Go for it, my love.

Suddenly, Cara's head jerks back violently, and she shudders, spasms, and screams in violation and pain, "STOP!"

Nic releases her mind in a panic and grabs her shoulders. "What did I do?"

Cara tries to get her breath back, slowly. She feels like her eyes are rolling around in her head. It takes a minute for composure. "I can't believe I'm going to say this...but I can SEE you in there." She saw a blurry vison of Nic's outline.

She stops to gather her thoughts. It's like you're in a room with those old rolling file systems that were popular in attorney offices and medical offices. The file cabinets were on tracks, and could be pushed along the tracks, one cabinet at a time, to get to a section and find a file. It was a system created to house a lot of paper files in a small amount of square footage.

Nic nods he understands her analogy. Cara looks to the group to confirm they understand. The kids look confused, so she adds, "They're mostly obsolete now. Many companies have moved to digital conversion of files and reduced their paper consumption in the name of going green."

What Nic just did felt like he ran into her brain and started slamming all those files along the tracks, yanking file folders out of their sections, and throwing them into the air in a crazy mess. Looking apologetically at her concerned husband, she blurts, "You just raped my mind." There is a collective gasp around the room, but Jake places his hand against the small of her back.

Nic needs to go back in slower and treat it like a file room. Open the door. Turn on the light. Look at the catalog showing where the files are, how they're organized, by alphabet, chronologically, or by emotion. Then slide the cabinets gently along the tracks until he finds what section he wants to be in. Once there, he should skim the sides of the files until he locates the exact one he's looking for and slip it out of its resting spot.

Cara looks at Sasha, who at this point is hiding behind Reed acting like he had nothing to do with the revelations that have taken place this morning. Pointedly, and with some indignation, Cara narrows her eyes at him and barks, "Don't think you're getting away Scot-free here. My handler missed my ability to read thoughts and emotions. Where were you all this time that Nic was doing the same and reading memories, as well." Sasha and Reed both inhale sharply, sinking down in an attempt to avoid her barbs.

Turning back towards her husband, satisfied Sasha is suitably chastised, she asks, "Nic, ready to try it again?

"You sure? You scared me before."

She can feel Nic's concern. She tries to allay his fears. "Don't sweat it. It was just a shock. That's all. Hell, they are my private memories and you violated them. That doesn't happen every day, babe. You're in a lot of them, anyway." She winks at her husband trying for levity but not really feeling it.

"Just talk me through it so I know each step of the way I haven't caused any discomfort."

They clasp hands, again, as Nic enters her mind. "I see you in there, she says." Gently this time, he draws open her memory. "Good, door's open." Suddenly her memories appear to illuminate. "Oh, pretty with the lights on. See the catalog?" Cara asks.

"Yes, organized by emotions, that's how you catalog them," he confirms.

"Decide which emotion." It's the strangest phenomenon to watch your husband's physical manifestation appear in your mind. He's standing in what looks like a file room, studying the cabinets, zeroing in on a subdivision. "Good, pick something out from that section." Slowly fanning through, he stops at one memory from the beginning of their courtship. "Nice skimming, my love. Open it and look inside."

Cara suddenly moves her hands to Nic's face. He does the same thing until they're holding each other, gazing directly into each other eyes as the memory plays out in her mind with him.

Sasha jumps down to them. "Tell us what you're doing."

Nic raises his eyebrows. "Not sharing, that's what we're doing." He tilts his head to look at her. "I didn't know that," he delivers with such emotion.

Cara leans in and places a soft kiss to his lips. "Now, you do."

Reed squats down next to them. "Find another memory, one you can share with the group. Get sentimental later, please."

"Reed!" Cara cautions, "These are MY memories. They are all sentimental and PRIVATE!"

Jake steps back in and pushes Reed aside. "Cara's right, back off." He stands up, looming over Reed and Sasha and places his hands on his hips. "I am still very disappointed with the two of you. I suggest neither of you do anything to piss me off," Jake threatens. Both men slink slowly away from her and Nic.

Nic chuckles at Jake's protection of them. He leans out and grabs Sasha by the ankle to prevent him from getting too far. He understands neither man meant any harm. And he comprehends why Reed needed to explore this, and quickly.

He gives Sasha his 'I forgive you' face. "Sash, I guess it's what I've been doing all these years without knowing it."

It's understandable his mind didn't recognize his talent as anything but intuition. It's overwhelming to consider the alternative. He's performing these processes at a rapid pace, most likely always scanning, and calculating without even realizing it.

"I see now how I've been able to track and trace people so well. I guess I was reading their memories, at least their short-term memories."

Sasha draws closer to him and drapes his arm over Nic's shoulder. "Like in Berlin yesterday morning. You knew to go see Olaf, yet you didn't know the story of Cara and Olaf...but I did."

In Cara's case, when she is in a confrontation, she sees the intent before it happens. She aims her gun before someone's hand reaches for his or her pistol, because she can read their commitment like she did with Reed earlier. The difference being Reed isn't a real threat. He had to build the image of hatred and loathing in his mind for Cara to see it and react. His conflicted emotions caused her confusion, but in the field, it's very clear to her. Targets and adversaries have lethal resolve, and she knows it.

Cara also knows when to extend compassion to an adversary. She can sense their hesitation and unease. She can distinguish possible friend from foe, like she'd done with Olaf, Lucien, and countless others, which earned her the respect of many agents in her field.

"With you, Nic, someone's memories determine their patterns. You know which way someone's going to swing at you, based on the patterns you see. You're processing those patterns at an alarming rate, but essentially, it gives you the advantage that Cara has, knowing intent," Sasha states, confirming Nic's thoughts.

Sasha adds, "Again, I'm sorry that Reed and I felt this course of action was the quickest way to confirm our suspicions."

"Are you going to tell me I'm a cheater, too?" Nic glowers at the man he has considered a brother since he was just a boy.

Sasha ignores the glare and turns to scowl at Reed, instead. "No, and neither of you are cheaters. It's a poor choice of words. You have gifts, and you've used them to your advantage. It doesn't matter if you utilized them with or without knowledge of it."

Sasha stands in an attempt to be closer to eye level with Jake. He focuses his mind on him before stating, "This is no surprise to you. You suspected Nic and me of having gifts. Somewhere along the way, you began to suspect Cara, too." There's some accusation in Sasha's tone.

"You and your new buddy have thrown down the gauntlet. I hope you're both prepared for the full repercussions," Jake replies with ice.

CHAPTER 3

CARA'S FEELING MUCH BETTER. SHE stands and stretches her back out. She walks around some furniture towards where Reed is just rising from the floor. She flicks her boyfriend in the head. He yelps and grabs her hand, pulling her into a hug as he whispers his apologies in her ear. She pulls away and seductively runs her fingertips down his chest before punching him in the stomach. "And you have the gall to accuse me of melodrama."

Reed is hunched forward, wincing, and placing his hands over his crotch, knowing that's her next target. Cara shakes her hand out because Reed's abs are rock hard, and now her knuckles hurt.

Nic, meanwhile, is up and making his way around Sasha and Jake, who are still glaring at each other. He pulls her away from Reed and toward the back window wall where their children are seated.

Nic, the reason Reed started all this is because it made more sense the kids would be targeted because of our gifts, not because of our skills. He was trying to determine if that was the motive. Also, he knows Mia and Max 'heard' your humming.

Cara mia, it's the reason I made my way closer to them. I'm liking this new form of communicating, by the way.

Knowing exactly what her husband wants her to do, she responds, *Max first, on three.* Simultaneously, Nic and Cara reach out and grab their son.

"No way, stop it!" Max yells trying to resist. Cara and Nic hang on long enough to get an answer to their suspicions. But before they can process their reaction to Max, Cara sees Mia jumping off the couch to flee.

Get her!

Nic grabs Mia by the nape of her neck while Cara reaches for her arm. All four of them are now linked together, physically. Mia is struggling to wiggle out of their grasp. Any onlooker might view the scene as child abuse.

Mia screams, "HELL NO!" and suddenly Cara is physically thrown onto Max's lap, except no one has pushed her. Nic is yanked hard ripping his grip from Mia, causing him to lose his balance. He manages to stay on his feet, struggling to maintain his hold on her. Small trickles of blood run down Cara, Max and Nic's noses.

As if someone hit the pause button, none of them moves, speaks, or even breathes. Then, Nic grabs Mia by the neck again, and yanks her hard out of the room towards the Owner's Suite.

Cara is stunned, still on her son's lap. Both are unmoving. The rest of the room finally reacts. Jinx goes running for a box of tissues, while Sasha and Reed lunge for Cara and Max. Sasha plops down next to Max while Reed kneels before them. Taking the tissues from Jinx, Reed removes some for Sasha while he takes a few to wipe Cara's nose. Sasha gently cleans Max.

There's still no communication until Cara breaks the silence. "What was that?"

Max looks up at her and sighs, "Obi Wan, the Force is strong in the girl."

This brings a slow smile to her face. She repositions herself slightly off her son, but pulls him in for a tight hug, taking the opportunity to get physical, having abandoned this contact long ago when the kids stopped letting her. She runs her hands over his beautiful face before...

Max, are you okay?

Yes, Mom, I'm fine, but my head feels weird, and I have a little headache. How about you?

Same thing. Mia did this to us?

Yup.

You knew?

His head slowly shakes. *Not about this little trick of hers, no. Mom, please don't take this the wrong way, but I don't like having you in my head. It's freakish. Like when we catch you and Dad sucking face.*

She snorts out loud. *You mean it's too intimate for your mother to be here? I understand, let's use our words. But Max, everyone is going to hear the rest of our discussion.*

Taking a deep breath, Max responds, *I am prepared for the disappointment, Mom.*

Drawing him closer to her by pulling his head to her neck, she inhales his maturing scent. *Dig in deeper inside my head, Max. You might be surprised.*

Argh, no thanks, I'll take my chances. He pulls away from her, looking for space.

Ignoring his attempt, Cara cups his cheeks and looks him straight in the eyes. *Max, always remember how much I love you. You will always be my beautiful baby boy. Nothing you could ever do would change that. Nothing.*

Cara rises from Max's lap but sits next to him. She inhales deeply before speaking. "Jinx, can..." Jinx is at Cara's side with a glass of water and 4 Advil. "Did I...?"

"Yes, you did, but I can recognize the difference in my head, now. It's fine." Jinx hands them the pills and water.

Cara knows Max is uncomfortable, but everyone is looking for answers so she starts, "Max and Mia have been communicating telepathically for as long as they can remember. But you don't do it as often now?"

"No, a few years ago it got weird being in each other's minds, so we only use it if we need each other or... to talk in front of you or Dad, mostly."

"You have extended each other privacy," Cara says making a statement. Max can read thoughts and feelings like her, but he's also capable of his father's talent. Max can read some memories. "Can you read past the short term and into the stored ones?"

"Sometimes, yes, it seems to depend on the person," Max replies with some anguish in his voice. His eyes are downcast.

Sasha places his hand on Max's leg to comfort him. As if reading the need, Reed places one hand on Max's other leg and wraps his second hand around Cara's calf. Cara pauses and ponders, her head tilting to one side. She sensed a tiny jolt of energy. She shakes her head slightly and looks to Jake.

Jake slowly nods to Cara and says, "Yes." Again, as if he knew what she was thinking. She nods back in understanding, but Sasha and Reed are confused by their exchange.

Cara continues, not addressing the small side interlude, "Max has been utilizing his talents in a not so discreet way these last few years... haven't you?"

19

Max lowers his head. "Yes."

Cara inhales, "You investigate people's thoughts, and then give them what you think they want to hear or feel. You do it a lot with girls. You scan them and come on as their 'fantasy' boy."

"You use it to be a player!" Sasha exclaims, grabbing Max by the head in more of a congratulations than a reprimand.

"Sasha! No encouragement required here, please," Cara scolds.

She attempts to parent her son by explaining what he's been doing isn't appropriate on so many levels, but she does understand at his age why he would be tempted. He must appreciate, though, having a girl like him based on a façade, isn't how relationships should develop. Girls should like him for who he truly is.

Max looks at his mother with disdain. "I am not an idiot, Mom. Having a relationship with them isn't what I want at the moment."

He admits he's taking advantage of this added talent. It gives him the competitive edge, especially playing sports. Max scans everyone on the field; knows what their next move is and what their strategy is going to be. "It's why I'm so good at everything. I WANT to win, Mom. Is that unfair?"

Cara is momentarily at a loss and looks to Sasha for help. Sasha seems to understand and takes over. "Ah, my sweet Westley. There is a time to be Westley, and there is a time to become the Dread Pirate Roberts. But you cannot be the pirate all the time. Sometimes you can even be both, but always, you must be sweet Westley."

Reed interrupts, "Is this *The Princess Bride* thing again?" Cara nods. "Okay, I get it, now."

Sasha continues, "Do you understand the difference, Maximillian?" Max nods solemnly. "Do you have the grid like your father does?"

"No, but Mia does. It's what makes her so smart and…crazy," Max replies while rolling his eyes.

Cara suddenly has her own moment of illumination. She looks to Jake, who is already in motion, walking towards his son. Elijah, who is sitting quietly on the other side of her, has not uttered a sound since this whole reveal began. Jake moves behind him and places a hand on Elijah's shoulder. Eli shudders a bit at the touch.

Knowing Jake wants her to lead the questioning, Cara turns to the boy. "Sweetie, have you seen Mia's grid?" Eli nods. "Do you have a grid, too?"

After a hesitation, Elijah nods. "Do you and Mia speak telepathically with one another?" A slow look moves across Eli's face before he finally nods an affirmative. Her eyes bolt up to Jake's.

Jake comes around to kneel in front of his son. "Eli, can you read thoughts and memories?"

Elijah speaks his first words of the day. "No, just Mia's, but sometimes I can get some images from others, like Cara described yours, opaque... muted," he confesses quickly.

All Jake has to say to that is, "Interesting."

Cara asks Max, "Can you speak to Eli?"

Max and Eli glance at one another, before Eli responds, "I speak to Max through Mia. We need her to facilitate the path. We can't do it alone."

Jake considers the phrase as he repeats, "Facilitate the path."

Cara looks back to Eli. "She just did that for you and Max? She's in your head right now?"

"Yes, she's frightened in the other room with her dad and needs comfort," Eli admits, reluctantly.

Cara immediately sends a short transcript of their conversation to Nic. She isn't even sure how she's done it, but the need for him to know seemed to 'facilitate' the expertise.

Nic responds immediately, *Got it. I'm trying to be delicate, but this IS MIA, you know. I'm not getting shit from her. She's getting a piece of my mind over the charge she threw at us, though.*

Cara smiles and thinks aloud, "Facilitate, I like the terminology, Eli. It's appropriate."

Jinx jumps up and states, "I'm starving. I'm ordering pizzas and salads for lunch. We can do a healthier dinner, agreed? And no Cara, I didn't 'receive' that from you. My stomach growling told me that." She struts out of the room.

After Carter returns from picking up their lunch order, he and Jinx start spreading everything across the kitchen island as a buffet. Having decided the boys had been interrogated enough, the rest of the group is seated at the kitchen table with the two boys standing, waiting impatiently for the food.

Nic and Mia arrive. Appearing worn and haggard, Nic tells the boys and Mia to fix a plate with some salad, take a pizza, and go downstairs to eat at the bar. They are relieved by their dismissal. Carter joins them, following the kids' lead.

The adults fill their plates and eat at the table. Jake has opened the bottles from earlier and Jinx has put out wine glasses. The bottles are passed around, but still, no one wants to communicate.

It's Sasha who finally breaks their occupied silence with, "Nic, we should talk about what we learned while you were gone."

Nic waves him off. "No need. Cara sent me a transcript while I was with Mia."

Reed puts his slice of pizza down quickly. "You. Did. What?"

Cara only shrugs. "It seemed prudent at the time, and I'm not sure how, but the ability to do it just came to me. Like I typed a quick text message and sent it off to Nic."

Jake saves her. "Now that Cara's brain has processed her abilities on a conscious level, the new neuropathways will start forming at an alarming speed. All brains have the capability; Cara's will do it on her level with her gifts, though. Nic will have the same thing happen, but with Nic's brain the new abilities will get a position on his grid. His brain is organized that way, where Cara's is...scattered like most folks."

"Scattered?" Cara accuses.

"Sorry, little darling, but you can't have everything," Jake mumbles to her.

"Jake, were you and Cara communicating during the Eli discussion?" Jinx asks with a bit of accusation in her tone. "You seemed to be."

Cara answers, "Not really. Like I did with Nic's grid, I sent a picture of my thoughts to Jake. And I get small snippets of Jake's thoughts back."

Jinx appears confused. "But you weren't touching him like before."

Cara doesn't need to anymore. She can identify Jake's thread in her mind and simply tap and send. It's reminiscent of a text message on a phone; if the phone was like the two cans and string game they played as children, as her kids would say, "like a hundred years ago."

Jake is very closed off, more so than the rest of them, but she suspects, like Jake has, they all have some talent. Cara does not have a grid of organization in her mind, but she is processing all this new information at an alarming rate of speed, even for her.

"Like you, Reed." Cara points to him with accusation. Reed cocks that one eyebrow at her in question and concern. She stops to take a sip of wine. "You and I have always done the thing with our foreheads when we're in distress. I've always thought it strangely intimate, and now I understand why."

THIS I want to hear. Her husband murmurs into her mind.

Shut up, you.

Reed considers this for a moment, "Are you asking me what I feel when we do it?" Cara nods. Reed appears to be thinking hard about this.

She truly senses Reed's emotions right at this moment. He loves the intimacy they share. There's a special bonding between them when they connect, but he's uncomfortable discussing it with the group. Squaring his shoulders, he tries, "It is strange. Like we're sharing something...not just you giving, but me providing...there's involvement by both of us... but it feels..."

Watch it, Reed. Nic's threat shoots into her brain.

Shut up you, again. Her husband's constant jealousy is muddling her sonar.

"It feels...enlightening?" Reed finally gives up.

"Yes, that's what I feel. Like we've resolved something and found closure. It's like healing," she confirms.

"But I don't hear your thoughts when we do it," Reed adds.

"Nor do I hear yours, but I'm certain it's more of an emotional exchange between us, empathic versus telepathic. And we have always had it. It was our connection to each other from the start. How I was able to manipulate you. I took advantage of your emotions."

"That's harsh," Jinx chimes in.

Cara's not feeling particularly harsh. Maybe she should have used Eli's word. She facilitated her need for Reed years ago when they first met. And now, she's feeling the beginning of complete acceptance for what has transpired. As traumatized as she felt earlier, the discovery isn't so shocking after all. Like an epiphany. All the jigsaw puzzle pieces are falling into place. All those times, she thought she was weird and a little unhinged for sensing things about people. Her aversion to spending too much time in large groups or keeping most people at bay. It's been enlightening. Reed's right. It's an illumination.

Narrowing her eyes on her boyfriend, Cara confesses, "But, Reed, you have facilitated, as well. You have been on the receiving end just as many times. It's why I don't feel I'm being harsh."

Everyone resorts back to silence at this small admission. But Reed breaks it with, "I'm beginning to see where this is going, and I'm not sure I'm ready to accept it. You think I possess this empathy talent, don't you? You think on a subconscious level, I have used it towards my career."

Cara rises from her chair and slowly approaches Reed. She takes his head in her hands and lowers her forehead to his, gently. They remain locked in this position for a minute before she releases his head and brings her face back just inches away from his. "I don't *think* you used it…I know you did," and she walks back to her chair to start eating again.

Their table companions have stopped eating and are sitting with their eyes darting between her and her boyfriend. Reed is watching her consume food. His expression is blank. When she's had enough, Cara puts down her fork and goes for the wine glass.

After taking a sip, she looks back to Reed and states with conviction, "You and I, sweetheart, we are brilliant *together*. Me, alone, not so much… at least not in the same way. Why is that? Because *you* are the master manipulator. *You* are the Spin Doctor with a premiere PhD in it. *You* are the big idea man. Maybe, all I did was pull those ideas out of your scattered mind for you as an assist, so to speak."

Getting up and back into his face, Cara adds, "Think about it, my dearest friend, think long and hard, back over these past 25 years. You will see the truth in my words. And when you do, you'll see *you* are a bigger cheater than I am!"

Sasha interrupts before anyone can react, scolding Cara and Reed. "Stop using words like cheat, advantage, manipulate or use. You need to refrain from any of that kind of talk. None of us has done that. We are all emotional right now and it's dictating our responses. More importantly, there are the children to consider. They don't need to feel guilty for their talents." Sasha, as usual, is the calm, clear voice of reason.

"Wise words, Sasha, I agree," Nic adds before turning his attention to her and Reed. "Can you two conclude your lover's quarrel and kiss and make up, please?"

This makes both Cara and Reed chuckle. They lock eyes on each other and smile. Reed reaches for her hand and squeezes it. All is forgiven. It's always been that easy between them.

Cara turns her attention to Jake. "Can you explain the touch thing now? What happened with Max and Elijah? I know you felt it earlier when Sasha, Reed and I sat down close to Max because I sent you my feelings."

Jake puts down his fork and peers at all of them. His eyes land and fix on Reed, though. He's sensing Reed wants to take back what he's unleashed today.

Reed stares back at him on full alert, preparing for another confrontation.

Jake breaks the staring contest and addresses Cara's question. "Some people possess the ability to harness energy. They amass it and expend it into different outlets. They may not show outward signs of this talent. Take me for instance." He can't read minds or thoughts or feelings per se, but he does have the ability to harness the energy, or so he's been told. "People with visible talent like Cara, Nic, and the children may or may not have the ability to stockpile the energy needed to use their talents for long periods."

Until they try to do it, they won't know for sure, but by touching someone who's a collector or enhancer, the gifts will increase. It's a power boost, simply stated. When Sasha and Reed touched Cara and Max, they sent a surge of something extra. This rush can manifest itself in different ways. In this case, they sent calming comfort to Cara, and that's the feeling Cara sent Jake. It was the added boost of warmth she and Max needed at that moment.

"But how did they know to send that particular energy to us?" Cara asks him.

His knowledge in this particular area is limited. "I'm not sure if you facilitate the energy yourselves into what you need it to be at the time, or if we're already sending it in a specific form."

Nic jumps in, his mind always processing on that grid Jake is envious of. "Jake, all that added energy, is that why Cara and I had a breakthrough today? I mean versus never before? All of us together in the great room with all the extra energy boosts?"

Jake sits back in his chair like he was pushed. Nic hit the nail on the head. It's exactly what he was just thinking about. Reed. He must be the missing link. This is the first time they've all been together with Reed. The Director's reputation precedes him. Jake's guessing that Reed stores a massive amount of energy. He reflects on the stories he has heard, some he witnessed firsthand, of the exploits of the Reflex and the White Night. They truly were quite the Duo. Not in the same way as the Dark Angel and the Widow Maker. Less lethal but more cunning. Cara is correct; together they are brilliant, maybe more so now than ever before. People still talk about the things the Duo could make you believe.

Jake points at Reed. "It's the Director. He's never been with all of us together." He explains his rationale and a lively discussion ensues regarding the Reed addition to the group, and how the odds favor him being the catalyst to the breakthrough.

Even though everyone is talking about him, Reed isn't listening. He can't fathom the notion that he, more so than any of them, can be powerful. He's still contemplating the empathic notion Cara threw at him, and the idea he used it to enhance his career. He hates that she's right. Worse, now Jake is implying the reason he and Cara were such an effective team is because of their combined gifts and his power. He is a fucking big, fat cheater.

Reed feels a foot knock against his. What the hell? He knows just from the touch it's Cara's. He looks up to see her give him two signals. The first is their 'I have your back' signal, followed by their 'love you, always'.

Cara gives him a big, warm smile. She can feel his guilt and self-doubt from across the table. She knows he's questioning their antics over the years. Sasha is right about it not mattering. So, what if all their successes were aided by a few gifts? Doesn't take away the successes. The conversation has now turned to Nic and Sasha and the energy they may have been providing each other during their missions as a team, but Cara's eyes are still wholly focused on him. There's the start of a small tingling up his spine. An awareness of something to come.

The tingling works its way into his brain to settle in one spot. He shuts his eyes for a moment. The prickling sensation has the feel of a mild ocular migraine. He can almost see a sparkly spot on his frontal lobe. The spot suddenly comes alive, and he can feel a torrent of respect and faith pass through his mind, like the hand of God just anointed him.

His eyes fly open, and Cara is staring intently back at him.

Cara had tried something with Reed's thread. Her thread to him is thicker and more pronounced than her connection to Nic. It's the thickest filament in her mind. The thread has a funky, shiny element woven into it. Continuing to ignore the conversation around her, Cara tapped Reed's thread and sent over all the respect she has for him. She was rewarded when with a jerk of his body, Reed's eyes opened and locked onto hers.

She can only smirk at him and sneak a wink when she suddenly feels an overwhelming sense of being loved. Thinking it's Nic, she turns her head towards him, but he's still engaged in conversation. Then she spies Reed's eyes still on her. He smirks and winks right back.

She snickers. Her boyfriend has found her thread in his mind and figured out the trick.

What the hell is going on over there? Nic interrupts.

She quickly sits upright. *Nothing, just experimenting.* She stops playing with Reed's thread and refocuses on the conversation.

Jake is correcting Nic about the use of the phrase 'shared talent' when describing his relationship with Sasha. "You can't think of it as one taking from the other. Think of the relationship as more symbiotic. With you and Sasha it's still unclear. But there is something there, trust me, I've seen you two together often enough, and it's a thing of great beauty. We just need to explore more with Sasha."

At this suggestion, Cara can see Sasha stiffen and for the first time, she feels his apprehension clearly. Needing to quell it, she shouts over to him, "Hey, Broody, don't be alarmed. No one is going digging in your head. Only when you're ready. But until then, just enjoy the ride." She winks at him but he's still brooding. Cara takes a piece of pizza crust and throws it at his head. He catches it with those quick reflexes of his and puts it in his mouth.

Sasha turns to Jake after he's chewed the crust. "This energy thing is power, and the power can be conveyed when necessary to another source?"

"Yes," Jake responds, "power fuels power."

Cara is reaching for her wine glass, but with those words her hand jerks and she knocks over her glass, sending the remaining contents across the table. Meanwhile, Reed lurches out of his chair so abruptly, it falls to its side, and he stumbles over it. Cara is unmoving and unblinking, while Reed is fumbling in his pocket for his phone like a crazy man. Nic, understanding the situation immediately by reading Cara's thoughts, grabs her by the shoulder and leaps right into her mind.

Her head is rocking back and forth in rapid sequence and Nic's face is inches from it. Within seconds, Nic has released Cara, and is yelling at Reed, who is flipping through his phone to find a number, "It's over 90%, Reed!" Reed finds the number he's looking for and rushes out the back door into the garage, his phone on his ear.

"Now, what the hell is going on?!" Jinx screams.

Cara is just sitting there in shock. The quick violation of her memories, coupled with the memory itself, too much to process. Nic takes her hand and announces, "I believe we may have just identified a prime suspect."

CHAPTER 4

CAUTIOUSLY, CARA RISES FROM HER seat. Her face is set, and her brows furrowed. Nic's hand is still in hers. She releases it, and walks deliberately towards the garage door. Nic is following her, but she turns and stops him with her hand up. Purposefully, she places her hand on Nic's chest. His body shudders with the touch that sends intense emotion through his mind.

You are connected to Reed. There is accusation in his mental voice. *These are his emotions. You can do that now?*

I located his thread, earlier.

Seemingly resolved and back in control, he offers, *Baby, based on his emotions, my calculation is 100%.*

I know. Please go ahead and tell the others the story. She and Reed never gave Nic the details on the plane. But he was able to pull her entire memory of the first couple months of her relationship with Reed. *I need some alone time with my boyfriend.*

I understand. It's all coming full circle.

Nic turns back to the gang sitting at the table expectantly waiting for an explanation. He will need to tell them the whole story for them to understand. He shifts his head back to the now closed garage door hoping neither Reed nor Cara will have an issue with their first interaction being discussed. He can assume Jake does not know the story but wonders if Jinx is even aware of the details.

Inhaling deeply, Nic heads back to his chair at the kitchen table. He pours himself some red wine and begins. "Just before Cara turned 20 years old, one of her sorority's housemates was raped at knife point on campus coming back from a frat party. Cara found her on the ground in shock. Unbeknownst to Cara, this was the third rape with the same MO on campus."

Looking around the table he can see three sets of big eyes watching him. He lowers his voice so he can't be heard by the kids. "Reed was an analyst in the FBI Hartford office at that time. They sent him to UConn to interview witnesses. Cara was his third witness, and she basically grabbed all his files and started reviewing them. Then she blackmailed him to let her assist on the case or she would tell his boss that he let her see the files." This gets a nervous chuckle from the group because despite the horrid subject matter, it's so Cara to do that.

Reed, being young and still a bit inexperienced agreed and worked with her to develop possible profiles for the rapist. "When a fourth rape occurred, the Hartford office sent Reed in undercover as a collegiate. Cara decided he would be her boyfriend from Harvard as his cover. They were both sure the rapist was a frat boy."

Jinx interrupts his story with a scowl on her face. "This is how they met? Why do I not know this story? Those little bitches." She leans back in her chair waiting on him to continue.

Nic explains how they attended frat parties as a couple for a few weeks. On the fifth weekend, Cara decided Reed should do his own mingling at each party so as not to appear connected to Cara. On that weekend, a fifth rape occurred. Except this rape had an additional element. The victim was raped at knife point by a masked man, but the man used the tip of his blade to carve the words, "POWER FUELS POWER" on the victim's abdomen.

He also spoke to his victim for the first time. The rapist kept repeating, "You are not her. I must find her." The team involved in the investigation couldn't come up with any additional leads on the words carved, or his comments.

The latest victim resembled Cara, so much so, they were mistaken for each other on campus. Reed believed Cara may be the actual target, but he did not share his hunch with his team, only with Cara. Of course, Cara pretended to disagree. Still, she decided they should break up and attend subsequent parties as singles. If this guy was after her, she wanted to be the bait.

There's a collective gasp around the room. Sasha whisper shouts, "Bait? An untrained civilian?"

Jake just shouts, "Reed let her do that?"

It is Jinx who comes to Cara's rescue. "Really guys? Since when have any of you been able to talk Cara out of anything when she sets her mind to it?" They all lower their heads in submission. "That's what I'm talking about! I get it. She placed Reed in either a win/win or lose/lose situation. She has always done that to him. Mostly, it's win/win, so she gets away with it."

The more he understands his wife's relationship with her boyfriend, the more he feels sorry for Reed. The man has taken the brunt of Cara's abuse all these years. In retrospect, Nic got off easy. Before he can reflect further on his relationship with his wife, he notices she and Reed have come back in through the garage door and are headed to her office.

Figuring it's time to get to the climax of the story he continues, "Cara announced to her sorority sisters she broke up with Connor. The first night they went to a frat party separately, Reed flirted with girls and danced, while Cara drank and danced with groups of other girls."

Apparently, Cara was approached by a young man who asked to dance with her to a slow song. As soon as she placed her arms on his shoulders, she sensed a threat. She spied Reed on the other side of the room and made sure he was watching her. He had many girls around him, but she was pretty sure he saw her dancing.

When the boy, who introduced himself as Ed Grotto, asked if she would go to the backyard with him to get more ice for the house, Cara followed. She had a feeling this innocuous, shorter boy was hiding something. But his explanation for being the "ice duty" frat house guy made sense.

Meanwhile, Reed lost sight of her and panicked. He knew she would not wander upstairs, so he checked the first floor than asked if anyone saw Cara. He was told she went outside with Ed. As he went through the back door, he unholstered the gun hidden in his boot.

When Cara and Ed approached the large ice cooler, Ed suddenly produced a knife and pointed it at Cara. With a lunatic calm Ed said, "It's you. I've been looking for you all this time. All the other girls were mistakes. You are my power and you, alone, will fuel me."

Reed was close enough to see the knife and hear Ed talking. He wasn't sure how to approach. Should he grab Ed from behind, or try to get a shot at him and risk hitting Cara? Before he could even calculate his advance, Reed watched as Cara stepped directly into Ed, pushed the arm with the knife away from her while throwing a solid punch with her right fist into his throat. Ed fell back a bit and Cara kicked him hard in the nuts. As he bent forward, he was met in the face with her knee.

Jake asks, "How did she know to do that?"

"You have met Tony, Cara's dad, right? The man trained his daughters early on. Taught them self-defense and took them to the shooting range. Tony is straight out of central casting for the *Sopranos*. I think he's a hoot. Cara has other ideas," Nic advises.

Before they can continue their questions, Nic tells them Ed was on the ground screaming "POWER FUELS POWER" when Reed got to them. Cara was holding the knife and threatening to cut off his balls. Reed managed to extricate the knife from Cara and wire tie Ed's hands behind his back. He called the incident in.

"By the time the shock wears off, Cara starts to worry. She doesn't want her family or anyone to know she took down Ed Grotto."

Again, Jinx interrupts him, "Because of her mother. Nina would have made Cara's life a living hell. She would have demanded Cara come home immediately and never leave the house. She would have made the incident all about her because that's what Cara's mother does. Her children are an extension of her, and they need to have their thoughts, feelings, and actions always approved by her." Jinx snorts, "Talk about central casting Italian mothers."

Funny, hearing Jinx say that about Nina gives Cara's complaints concerning her mother some credence. Nic always thought it a bit bratty of Cara to bitch about her mother, but he does see that Nina is all about herself. When they dine at Cara's family home, it is expected everyone compliments Nina on her cooking, her home, her efforts over the get together, her grandchildren, etc. It's always about Nina. She barely asks her children how they are doing. She only talks about how she is "getting along" with her life.

No wonder Cara let Reed take all the credit for the capture. Cara's relationship with her mom is a huge reinforcement of her keeping secrets mentality. She's never told either of her parents anything about her life then or now, for that matter. Admission of truth would only bring her grief.

Her rambling analogy back in Berlin about Pavlovian response and reaction to threats makes sense to him now. She is so accustomed to secrets. And because of their previous working relationship, of course she would go running to Reed instead of her own husband. The same applies to her family. In her mind the truth hurts, something reinforced throughout her childhood and adult relations with her parents.

And speaking of truth, Nic is not comfortable letting on he knows that particular successful capture was the catalyst for Reed's new position as Team Leader for the CIA. He will keep that secret for Reed to tell if he chooses. Nic only wraps up with, "Cara did testify at Ed's trial, and he was linked to all five rapes and an additional attempted sixth rape. He was indicted and sent to jail for life."

Grateful Nic didn't have any issues with what he saw in her memories from her first weeks with Reed, Cara walks out the garage door. Reed is immobilized, staring at his phone. The look of terror, frustration, anger, and guilt is evident on his face. The associated emotions are passing through to her, penetrating her mind.

Reed sees her, tilts his head slightly and says, "He's out. Been three weeks now."

"I know. I felt your reaction when you discovered this information."

"This is entirely my fault." He lets out a big, stuttering breath.

"No, it's the circle. It's time to come 360 degrees." Cara puts her hand out to him.

Reed takes it, reluctantly, and she begins to pull him into the house. They proceed back through the door, and as they pass the kitchen, they can hear Nic reciting the tale that altered their lives. They pay it no attention as Cara continues to lead Reed to her office at the front of the house.

Upon entering, she shuts the French doors and motions him to the sofa. She sits next to him, but there's a penetrating silence before they both hear the distant hum of voices from the kitchen.

"I just realized we never told the details during our recounting of the story to Nic on the plane," Reed thinks aloud.

"Nic could see the memory in my head and went in hard. He yanked it all out. His speed is amazing." Cara responds as if they're chatting about the weather. She looks forward and not at Reed.

"You knew you were always Ed's original target at UConn. All along. You knew that, didn't you?" Reed accuses. "Grotto altered his MO on the rapes right before his attempt with you. He etched those words into the abdomen of his final victim. 'Power Fuels Power'." Again, he accuses, "You knew."

At the time, the words meant nothing to her and Reed's investigation. They couldn't make heads or tails of the added twist in Ed's MO. It wasn't until Ed had her in the backyard, and he was shouting 'power fuels power' at her, she suspected he specifically wanted something from *her*. "Not originally, no, but I knew it wasn't just the connection to finding one of the victims that prompted my interest in the investigation. It was more. Then, when I met you, I don't know, I felt an opportunity."

Studying her for a moment, Reed's eyes sparkle with understanding. "You think the circle starts there with us, in that moment, in a campus police interview room."

"Yes. You have my thread, and Ed has my thread."

"Are you referring to this connection that allows you to read thoughts and feelings?"

"Can you see mine, now, in your mind?" Wrapping her hand around his wrist, she pulls gently.

Reed looks down at her area rug. For some reason he can't look at her when he confesses, "The sparkly one. It's my connection to you. But what is it?"

"The threads unite everyone, somehow. They bring us together." Cara has heard it referred to in science as a collective consciousness. Everyone is a part of it, but some people can see the actual threads. She could always sense the cohesion of those around her, but now, she can view it.

"So, it was fate driving us to meet all those years ago?" Reed questions, delicately.

Fate means a lot of different things to different people. Destiny, divinity, a calling, Cara doesn't know what it truly is, but some of the threads are much thicker than others, much more vibrant as well. "Best way to describe it is some people appear to be hardwired, while others are just coming in Bluetooth. You are hardwired to me, big time."

"You don't want me to feel guilty. I'm sensing or rather receiving that message from you," Reed whispers.

"Guilt is not a component of this. It's irrelevant. Anger, on the other hand, is acceptable." With this statement, Cara turns to Reed, her face radiating rage. "How did it happen? How was Ed released without your knowledge? It was the only promise I asked of you. I needed Ed Grotto to stay in prison; if he was released, I was to know immediately or prior to."

"There was always a standing order for me to receive any change in status on Edward Grotto. Last I checked, Ed wasn't up for parole until 2024. I'm being told, between a new warden and some State snafu, he was released. You said Ed has your thread. Do you have his?"

She is certain Ed has her thread because the past makes sense now. He was pulling the thread to try to locate her. He felt her presence on campus. He was getting so close at the parties, but just missing Cara. Ed could not have known how it worked, precisely. He just felt the pull, or the power. His body searching for the source; knowing he wanted it. He knew just enough to etch those awful words on the last victim's abdomen.

"Remember, he kept reciting it over and over when the police were taking him away. Is that when you realized you were always his intended target?" Reed questions.

Thinking back, Cara admits, "No. The words meant nothing to me. It was when we danced, back in the frat house. As soon as he touched me, I felt his connection. He did, too."

Reed is trying to contain his frustration with her. It's obvious, without even needing to say it. She always led him to believe he was crazy for thinking she was Ed's intended target. It's his turn to grab her wrist and tug. "This is one of those perfect examples of me knowing in my gut that I was right, despite what you said. So, you have his thread?"

Cara nods confused. "I can't recall it, though." She leans against him and sighs. She didn't understand any of this until much later, not until she first saw Nic. Somehow, with Nic, her subconscious and her conscious began to coexist in spots. She sensed Nic's thread strongly at first contact but didn't know it was an actual thing. Of course, their cliché fairy tale relationship has a rationale now. Really, all her relationships are making sense.

She did know she and Nic were different, somehow. Cara could always sense Nic's thoughts and feelings. And she suspected he could sense hers. "When I first saw Nic in Kabul, my thread to him pulled at me, obsessively, much in the way Ed's was pulling him to me."

"You're saying the thread claws at you like a madness?" he questions, interrupting her ramblings on the intense intimacy she has with her husband.

"Yes, it can."

Cautiously, Reed asks, "Were you meant to end up with Ed and not Nic?"

"No. I think the thread makes the power connection." To Ed, the connection manifested itself into something obsessive, sick, and disturbed. "Without knowing what gifts Ed has, it's hard to say what the actual connection was meant to be between Ed and me."

Baby, you know I've been in your head listening to this, right? Nic's voice doesn't surprise her.

Yes. I know when you're here, now. I kept you here for this purpose. Besides, I find it…soothing.

Oh, cara mia. When you're ready to return, everyone has questions, and I would like to try something with you.

She already knows what he wants to attempt. *I needed to take a moment to gather my emotions and get control over Reed's reactions flooding my body. Be there shortly.*

"What I don't understand is the timeline," Reed states, cutting into her mental conversation with her husband.

"Everyone in the kitchen is wondering as well. Ready to join them?"

"Before we go back," Reed confesses, while drawing her onto his lap, "you were right about the two-way street between us. Like you, with this newfound gift, I've never considered how or why I made the choices I did. How easy it is to ignore the gifts. Treat it like some sort of intuition."

Cara pulls Reed's forehead down to hers and then wraps her arms around him. "Connor, I'm sorry I lied about the Ed thing. I knew you would worry if I told you the truth and…you were leaving." After Ed's trial, he was moving away to a new job and the life he always wanted with the CIA. "I wanted you to have a fresh start. No worries, no guilt."

He pulls her face to his until they're nose to nose and whispers, "C, did you think I wasn't going to keep in touch?" Cara can only blink at him. She had no idea if Reed would move on with his life and only think of her occasionally, until he didn't think of her at all. "Sweetheart, I may have gone six weeks before I saw you, but how many times did I call after I moved to DC?"

Cara smiles at him and takes a swipe at his lips with her tongue. "Every night when you came home from work."

He grabs her chin, firmly. "And yet, you continued to let me think I was crazy with my Ed theory. You are just filled with secrets, and it's beginning to piss me off. You truly are the biggest pain in my ass."

Cara gives him a little headbutt. "Ready to solve a crime, Agent Reed?" This gets a big smile from him because he remembers when she first spoke those words to him 25 years ago.

CHAPTER 5

SASHA IS UP AND PACING when Reed and Cara arrive back in the kitchen. The chatter stops as everyone notes her entrance but not for long. The discussion immediately continues as Sasha reasserts his feeling the timeline is all wrong.

"Vlad was hired months ago, and Edward has been out for only three weeks on a technicality, which means he had no foresight. Hiring Vlad would've been futile unless he knew he was getting out. And, there's no money trail." Taking command, Sasha barks to Reed, "What do we have on Ed and his assets? Could he have funded the hit?"

Reed shakes his head. "Ed has nothing substantial. Nothing we can find. My team at Langley has already ascertained his financial info. Ed's phone records are being pulled as we speak, as well as all records of visitation. He did have use of the Internet once a week. And, of course, I have agents heading to the address Ed listed with his parole officer."

"They're not going to find him there. He is long gone," Nic states as if he already knows.

"I suspect as much, but it's worth the visit to collect any evidence. I should hear shortly on the outcome of the premises search," Reed advises.

"He isn't in this alone. You know that, right, Nic?" Cara inquires. She has some precognition of this fact. Plus, Reed received confirmation the pilots were roofied before their near fatal flight home the day before. And it was in Berlin they were drugged. The dinners and everything on the plane were clean. They did venture into the private terminal in Berlin for coffee and lunch. Analysts are looking for footage within the terminal.

"This is a coordinated effort by several people. I just can't make the connections between them. Is that what you're surmising?"

"Very strongly through my experience with Vlad," Cara tells him. It's so weird how much of this back and forth is going on in her mind with Nic, but they are speaking aloud so everyone else can hear.

"I'm accessing as much of his short-term memory as I can from my visit with him," Nic offers.

"You can do that? Go back before you realized your gift and still assemble information?" Sasha asks, shocked.

Based on the memory of their meeting, Nic can pull some info from the confrontation. It's not as clear as if Vlad was standing in front of him, but he did get some insight. Because of it, he wants to try something with Cara.

Sasha grabs Nic's arm. "I don't think that's a good idea."

"You know what I want to do?" Nic turns to his friend, surprised. "Because you have processed the options, or because *you* pulled it from my mind?" Nic only spoke to her, mentally, about his plan.

Sasha steps back from Nic, like he was pushed away. He ignores the questions and instead, he cautions Nic, "If you try to connect to Ed's thread, he may be able to re-connect to Cara. There is the high probability of it. She would be bait, once again."

She winces. After six weeks of investigating together, the connection happened the first weekend they attempted their new plan, separately searching for clues instead of as a team. Just like then, she knows she must be bait, again.

Cara notices the concern on the faces around her and decides to explain Nic's bait plan for this go around. Nic thinks he can go into her head to the memory moment when Ed touches her, and she feels his thread. From that instance, Nic believes he can follow Ed's thread back into his 1989 mind, or possibly into his mind now. It's probable a thread is a thread and is timeless.

With this revelation, Reed rises out of his chair. "I agree with Sasha, too dangerous."

Sasha rephrases, "I'm not saying it isn't an option, just not yet. First order is to establish whom Ed is working with. We must know who our adversaries are." It will change the entire equation to their favor if they can identify the targets. "Nic, please first think about what you and Cara can do to get those answers."

"Can you try something else for me?" Jake inquires, interrupting their current train of thought. "Can you scan an area?" He wants them to attempt to extend their talents, collectively, around the house and see if they can pick up anything out of the ordinary, anything malicious. "It is highly probable we are being watched."

Cara and Nic look at each other. With the added power boosts sitting around this table, it would be intriguing to try it. She offers, "I could cast out my sonar, with Nic reading the results on his grid."

"Let's do it," Sasha insists, going back to his seat at the table convinced this should be their next move.

Nic sits down motioning her onto his lap. She straddles him and points the rest of them to place their chairs closely around them. Once they're in a tight circle around her and Nic, she looks to Jake to direct the experiment.

"Let's try this in increments. Nic, you and Cara do your thing by yourselves, first. See what you accomplish. One by one, we'll add our support by placing a hand on each of you. It will direct the power to you, marginally," Jake decides.

Cara leans all in, putting her head on Nic's shoulder and traveling over his thread. *And there's that complicated mind. I've missed it.*

Welcome back. He nuzzles her neck.

I don't know if I can look directly at your grid, Nic. It's sort of disorienting for me. But if you tell me where I should focus during this exercise, I can do that. I just can't take it in all at once like you do.

I'm not sure where the information will place itself because we've never done this together, but if we're successful, I'll show you. I'm going into your head, but not into your memories just yet. Cara stiffens. *I'm in.* She didn't feel any discomfort this time. As a matter of fact, she's feeling quite the opposite. *Um, Nic? What are you feeling right now?*

Very turned on. He's moved on from nuzzling her neck to kissing her jaw.

Me, too! Is it because you are, or I am, and we're projecting it to each other? His hands on her ass draw her tighter to him. *OOHH, I do feel your physical arousal now, too.*

I think it's the intimacy of our minds together. And thank God you're sitting on my lap covering that physical arousal. It might be humiliating, otherwise.

Cara hides her face in Nic's neck to stifle a giggle. *Okay, back to work. You want to lead?*

Nic directs Cara to start by scanning out from the kitchen and let him play with that. *I can see what you mean about the four in the room with us.* Jake is sealed tight, and the other three are foggy. *But I can see their short-term memories fairly well and their feelings, just not their immediate thoughts.*

She notices Nic concentrating on her thread to Reed. It's hard not to. It's the thickest thread in her mind and glittery. She offers, *That one is Reed's.*

Now it's Nic's turn to stiffen. Very calmly he says, *I think I see too much of that connection. Can you tone it down? Reed's emotions are overpowering, and a source of future debate for you and me later, my dear.*

Duly Noted. How's that? She makes a concerted effort to block Reed's thread.

Better, thanks. Now, see if you can scan the kids downstairs. She located all three kids' threads earlier in the great room, but Carter and Far Guard are downstairs with them now. She has nothing on them. Deciding to push, she gathers Nic's strength and extends her reach.

Good, Nic praises, *and yes, the kids are like granite. Even more so than Jake. Carter's worried about what's happening up here, and Far Guard is happy he was fed.* She giggles because Far Guard is disappointed with the Ohio pizza. Which does suck compared to the East coast. *Focus, baby. Push out and see if you can read the FBI agents.*

Again, she draws power from Nic, pushing beyond the boundaries of the house. Now, she is not only getting all the feelings from in the room, and the thoughts from downstairs, but the minds of five agents outside.

Wow, holy input! Nic shouts as all the jumbled mess reaches them.

It's the overwhelming noise thing. Can you help me zero in?

He's working on something on his grid while he muses, *It's so different from within the house. You can hear all their thoughts. No wonder your mind blocked the talent at an early age. How the hell did our children handle this, Cara?*

Her stomach clenches. *I feel a 'bad mommy' moment coming on if we keep talking about it. Can we bench the guilty parent conversation for later, as well?*

Nic can clearly sense her distress, and it's not helping. *Cara mia, the kids are fine. Please don't stress.*

Jumping back and forth between his mind and Cara's, Nic is attempting to combine their gifts. He had the ability to organize his mental grid and add quadrants before, but with Cara's talent and boost, the ease and speed is remarkable. A new section is complete, but Nic is studying Cara's threads in her mind.

Besides the connection they have to each other, the other threads share a resemblance except for that one to Reed and her thread to Sasha. Nic jumps back into his own mind to identify his threads to the group. He can locate the one to Reed, but the thread doesn't share any resemblance to what Cara has to him. His thread to Reed looks like the ones to the others. Nic locates his thread to Sasha. That thread is the thickest of any of his.

Sasha's thread to him has some of the same coloring in it he observed in Cara's mind, but it's not identical. Nic focuses in on Sasha's thread. It appears to have a subtle vibration to it.

Refocusing on his new quadrant, he moves all the chatter she's receiving straight to his mind.

It's quiet! Did you do that? He instructs her to look at what he's done. *Are you using your GPS with some of the other talents to do this?* Poor thing. She's lost.

Something like that, he answers because he doesn't want to complicate this for her.

He moves back to Cara to ask her if she can take all their threads and hold them, mentally, at once. Treat it like pulling the strings and keeping them in her hand. Cara practices it while Nic assists her. She can do it, but it's like touching them all, versus holding them. More like keeping her mental fingertips on each thread. When he feels they have achieved the required result, Nic travels back to his mind to work on his new quadrant.

He has left Cara, alone, with mental fingers on all their threads, but he can hear her thoughts. She's comparing the marginal difference in each thread's energy. Oddly, despite her connection to him, it is Reed's thread emanating the clear energy boost. She's contemplating whether Jake's hypothesis about Reed is the rationale for that, or their years of history together. Wondering if the synergy she and Reed have mastered through their training could cause a thread to develop, or if the threads exist as is from inception. Cara can recall always having more energy when she was with Reed, from the very beginning. She even sleeps better when he's around.

Nic's trying to focus on the task at hand, but this new gift reveal is only making him more jealous. Getting back on topic, he asks Cara to keep her grasp on those threads as she makes her way to his mind. He's not sure she's going to be able to do it when he suddenly feels her presence behind him.

Good girl! You never cease to impress, baby. Now, watch the section just to the left of the GPS on my grid. I'm going to cue into each Agent outside, separately, so we can hear.

Cara busts out laughing while Nic chuckles.

Jake is getting impatient with the lack of conversation. "What the hell are you two doing?"

"Chill, Reacher," Cara scolds. "Nic and I had to get the mojo correct. We just got outside with the two agents in front of the house. And…let's say their conversation is enlightening."

"You can actually hear them talking?" Jake asks, excited.

"Yeah, they're discussing which of the two MILF's in the house is more fuckable," Cara offers as explanation for the laughing. "Is fuckable a real word?"

"What!" Jinx jumps up. "Wait…which of us is, you know, more fuckable?"

Nic responds they've decided Jinx has the nicer ass, but Cara's tits win and actually in the end, they want to do both. "Sorry ladies, it's a tie." At this admission, Jinx turns and starts shaking her ass in Cara's face. Cara slaps it. "Ladies, please, it's clear you both can get laid, can we move on?"

"Back to work, fine," Cara announces right before she and Jinx high five each other. As if there was any question either one of them could get laid. Men have been, and are still, very drawn to his wife. She has male clients hanging on her every word and making excuses to meet with her so they can spend time in her company. Heads turn all the time, but that never bothered him. He has always been proud she chose him, and is secure in their relationship. Well, except for Reed.

I heard all that.

Fuuuck. This mind reading may take some getting used to. He empties his thoughts and refocuses. There will be time, later, to address his concerns.

Once he's prepared, he instructs Cara to scan away from the house as far as she can. From there, they can start adding the others for energy one by one. She relays the info coming off Nic's grid. Neighbors are arguing on the right, on the left are not home. Across the street is very concerned about the black cars and scary looking men.

"Nic, you need to go see them and assure them. I've forgotten about our neighbors noticing the FBI boys outside," Cara admonishes him.

Wait. What? "Why can't you go, Cara?"

"Check the wife's memories, Nic!"

Nic zeroes in on Mrs. Landers particular thoughts. "Oh, eeewww, ummm, wow…" He's speechless.

Cara announces, "For our studio audience this afternoon, my friendly neighbor across the street has some interesting erotic fantasies of which *my* husband is the star." Guess there's no question he can get laid, as well. "That's why you get to go talk to them, Nic. Moving on down the street. How fast can you go?"

Feeling the strain on them, Nic makes a request. "I think we need Jake now, and see if we can scan with some more speed and accuracy." Then he adds, "Jake, can you empty your mind as much as possible and try to bring down your blocks? We promise not to pry." Jakes composes himself for a moment before placing a hand on Nic's shoulder and Cara's arm. "Cara, did you feel that?"

As soon as Jake touched them, they could feel the additional energy coming from his thread. Nic instructs Cara to take his thread and pull lightly to bring Jake into the collective. Cara does as he requested, and he can feel a very small part of Jake's consciousness enter.

Jake's body jerks, and his eyes grow wide. "Is this what you're seeing?"

Nic is ecstatic it worked. He coaches Jake to focus on the top left corner of his grid, and then follow the grid to the right to the next quadrant. Nic has the play by play on the street, and the dialog, coming through as images and texts. He is converting the thoughts Cara hears into texts so they can read them, as opposed to hearing the jumbled garb. It seemed more streamline.

"Nic, you are incredible! I can totally follow it," Jake states with true admiration.

Nic begins to slowly expand the scan area. He can tell by his wife's thoughts he's losing her on the play by play. "Cara, just focus on the threads in your mind and the scan only. Let me process from now on."

Cara is relieved she doesn't need to look at Nic's disorienting mind anymore. Attempting to mentally multitask, she heads her scan in the direction of the South half of the neighborhood with a portion of consciousness, while maintaining her fingers on the threads. The extra energy from Jake's thread does appear to add a boost to her own mental efforts. Cara is trying to get outside their neighborhood, figuring anyone watching them is likely to be outside the gates, closer to the shopping plaza. She can sense the further they go, the harder it becomes.

"Cara, more power, who do you want next?" Nic asks knowing they are slowing down.

"Reed, can you do the same thing as Jake? Empty your mind AND your emotions for me?" Cara inquires a little too harshly.

"Let it rip, C," Reed teases her as he places a hand on Nic's arm and Cara's shoulder.

Cara gives Reed's mental thread a gentle tug. As soon as she does, Nic and Jake gasp while her mind lights up like a Christmas tree, all circuits firing.

Reed feels an overwhelming dizziness, and he grips Cara's shoulder. Her hand comes down over his firmly, and her other hand grabs his leg. When she is certain Reed isn't going to fall, she pats his hand. "You okay, sweetheart?"

Before Reed can answer, Jake interjects, "That's some serious energy you got there, Director. I think our hypothesis about you is spot on."

Cara warns Reed she's going to try and connect him like she did for Jake so he can see. Jake has a grid but Reed doesn't. Just a fair warning to him, it may be disorienting. If it is, Reed's to let her know. She will keep him on her side of the scanning.

Reed squeezes Cara's shoulder and she pulls his thread a little more. "OH MY GOD! Holy shit! Where am I supposed to look?" His eyes are wide in panic.

Cara giggles out directions. The images and texts are scrolling fast. Nic and Jake are processing them. She feels vindicated she isn't the only one who can't look at that grid for long. "Look quick at the Supermind, then stay with me on my side."

"I see the images, but you're right, it's like watching the credits of a movie on fast forward," Reed admits, trying not to sound too drone. "Sorry."

"I can use the company, watch this instead." Cara brings him back to her and sends him the scan, which is strange in itself.

It feels like they are flying above the houses and plopping into each one. The thoughts of everyone they pass are over on the mind screen in Nic's mind, but Reed can sense the emotions as they travel. It's remarkable he can pull that from the scan. Trying to release his initial anxiety, he focuses on those emotions he's feeling.

"See the shopping plaza? That's my grocery store. I like it there. Everything is organized in the aisles, as it should be. There's always plenty of checkout lanes open and…"

Cara's yapping is disrupting Reed's concentration. "Shut up, C, and just drive," he teases her. "Wait. Can you pull to the left more towards… what's that big boxy building?"

"Movie theater."

"Head that way while you scan. I'm feeling something there," he instructs, sounding like the Director he is.

Aware that they made the longest leap with Reed's energy, Nic requests Jinx join them next. Wordlessly, Jinx saddles up in front of her husband and takes a spot on Nic's arm and Cara's leg. The group inhales collectively at her touch.

Reed must comment, "That's some fine hot ass energy you got there, Jinx."

Jinx thanks Reed for his sarcastic compliment, but she hesitates when Cara asks if she's ready. "Based on what you all are saying, I'm really intimidated by Nic's mind and what Cara's about to do."

Sensing her anxiety, Cara assures her it will be fine. She softly pulls Jinx's thread, hoping the transition will be easier. "I'm going to give you a quick peek at Supermind, and then bring you back…now," Cara warns.

"Jesus Nic, you're a hot mess! Jake, you can follow that?" Jinx shouts.

"Yes, my scatterbrained love, I can," Jake responds to his wife flatly.

"Almost through the plaza. Reed, how much further to the area you're getting something from?" Nic inquires.

"About 100 yards."

"Sasha, it's time. Ready, my friend?" Nic asks with some concern.

Nic wants Sasha to do the same thing, empty his mind, and then latch on. Cara will take it from there and throw him the moving picture. Sasha should try and stay with Jake and Nic for a moment. Cara can take him, afterwards.

Sasha stands behind Nic and places one hand on Nic's head and one on Cara's head. As soon as his hand lands on Cara's head there is a collective buzz. Her hair stands straight up. Jinx's hair does the same thing. Reed feels goosebumps spread across his skin and a charge shudder through him causing the scan to static out for a moment. Everyone is speechless for a full minute feeling the effect.

"My brother, you have always had an electric personality. Do you feel this?" Nic jokes.

Sasha says nothing but, "Cara, picture."

"Don't ignite big guy, it's coming. I'm sending you straight to Nic, though, tell me when you need to come back," Cara counters defensively. Reed can sense her struggle for Sasha's thread. It's distinctive and much more vibrant and colorful than the others. Whereas his thread has a metallic filament to it, Sasha's is iridescent. When she tugs it, the thread latches on, like a mental hand has grasped her mental finger. He can feel Sasha pass through her with such speed and force; Reed swears her hair swings with the momentum.

"Welcome to the show, Sasha. Let me explain..."

"I got it Nic, no explanation required," Sasha snaps.

Reed, Cara, and Jinx watch as Sasha migrates quickly and effortlessly through Nic's mind. He's moving from quadrant-to-quadrant sorting through it all, absorbing like a sponge. Cara has stopped scanning because she's enthralled by Sasha's ability to navigate and process Nic's grid so easily. Next thing they know, Sasha is back in Cara's mind returning to them of his own accord.

"Reed, show me the target you see," Sasha barks out. "Cara, I feel it too, skip everything, go right there. Better yet, let me."

"What the...did you just take the helm? How the hell did you... STOP!" Cara shrieks.

Sasha keeps the controls but ceases all forward movement.

Reed is correct about the location, but Cara's head is spinning from Sasha commandeering control from her. She needs Sasha to stop and proceed with caution. Cara can feel the man in the blue four door Camry parked North of the theater. He appears to be a blocker though, maybe, with his own gifts. She's getting a similar vibe to what she feels with her group. There is no strong connection between them to tap into. But she does see a faint thread extending from him to her. It's too weak and indistinct to pull, but she wonders if she can travel on it. She brings a part of her consciousness close to his faint thread to feel his emotions. "I'm getting malice and rage and..."

"Revenge," Reed offers.

Cara warns, "Nic, you need to be very cautious. Just you and I are going to get closer."

Nic refocuses in Cara's mind to mystery man's thread. She is going to try to travel it while pulling Nic along. She wants to attempt to invade and violate.

"Pull on my mark. Get everything you can from his mind, Nic. We can process it later. Reed, Sasha, see the thread he has connected to me? It's faint, but it's there. If you see it quiver, scream."

Nic and Cara covertly move along the thread. She isn't registering much in the way of thoughts, but the emotions are evident. She creeps forward pulling Nic along with her. Nic is beginning to access his memories.

"There's movement!" Sasha says abruptly.

Before Cara pulls out, Nic runs the thread and does a smash and grab. He snatches everything he can and takes it with him as Cara quickly travels off the thread.

"Everyone off," Cara yells.

The group removes their hands and Cara releases their threads. Her head falls back as if she was punched. Nic's head falls forward. Everyone appears a little disoriented, eyes dazed and hands trembling.

They start to back away, but she reaches out roughly for Sasha's shirt and pulls him back towards her and Nic. Holding him by the collar, she pulls Sasha's head in between them. "Guess we figured out *your* gift… Captain." She salutes him before pushing him away.

"I'm on it, Cara, pot of coffee coming right up," Jinx says with a mocking smile towards Cara before shaking her ass across the kitchen. Obviously, Cara only needs to crave coffee and poor Jinx is in action.

Nic gently tries to calm Cara's hair down with his hands. He gives up and leans in for a kiss, advising, "We should take a break, and then mind palace the smash and grab loot from the Camry man." Pausing for another deeper kiss, he pulls back to add, "That was impressive, my love."

It really did look like a smash and grab from inside Cara's mind. The fact Nic's calling it loot is even funnier. She rises to use the bathroom and get a hairbrush as she chuckles to herself, picturing a thief's black sack filled with memories.

Before she walks out of the kitchen, she spies Reed pulling Sasha aside, and stops to listen. "Argh, Reed, I know what you're about to say to me. What the hell? We're all getting way too intimate," Sasha says, disgustedly.

"What was I going to say?" Reed wants to know, but he whispers his request to Sasha.

"You were about to comment the six of us could take down a small country. And you're correct, we can. How fascinating would that be?" Sasha winks at poor Reed.

"Cara's right, you *are* the Captain." He salutes Sasha and runs up the stairs.

Of course those two particular men would already be contemplating political and borderline nefarious uses of their gifts.

CHAPTER 6

WHEN CARA RETURNS TO THE kitchen, Nic hands her a full mug of coffee as she passes by him heading towards Jinx. She gives the other woman a hairbrush and pats her head, thanking her for making the coffee.

Jinx still appears dazed as she rhythmically starts brushing her hair. She finally looks to Cara. "I'm feeling like the duh in our little evil franchise. Can someone explain to me what just happened, and how we were all in your brains?"

His wife's gaze rests on him and Nic gathers his thoughts before speaking. "Nobody was in my or her brains, per se. Cara combined some of her consciousness with all of yours. In doing so, she created a 'pocket', for lack of a better word, to store shared pieces of consciousness from each of you."

That's how they could see what the others were doing. Cara couldn't reach the people outside their bubble on her own. She needed the thicker thread connection and collaborative effort of this close group of friends inside the house to create a path to the outside.

That very faint connection they were able to make with everyone they passed after leaving the house, was obtained through what might be referred to as a weave of mankind's thoughts, a universal mindfulness. Scientists are calling it collective consciousness.

It's a term originally coined in 1893 by a noted Sorbonne sociologist, Émile Durkheim. Durkheim observed that people's beliefs, standards, and principles make up a shared way of understanding in the world, a collective consciousness. It's what binds individuals together to generate social assimilation.

Later, in the 1970's, scientists continued to develop the hypothesis of a human collective consciousness. And in 1998 a coalition of scientists developed the Global Consciousness Project. They set up and monitor a hardware network of random number generators that have been placed around the globe. They examine output before, during, and after significant worldwide events to measure for common emotional responses of large groups of unrelated people, thereby proving the theory of a global consciousness. Although many scientists have written opinions debunking the claims, the project received a significant boost when these generators registered a spike in activity during the 9/11 attacks.

This collective consciousness is mind-centric parapsychology, the concept of our brainwaves interacting with the physical world. The concept is not groundbreaking. Similar to meditation and prayer, it's the theory of mind over matter, of using the infinite power of the brain to overcome limitations. Lately, people refer to the spilling of positive energy as manifesting. It's not an original idea. It's been around since the dawn of man. Every human being is doing it without realizing his or her thoughts are reaching a common denominator. They are all using willpower to influence reality.

As to how everyone is connected, he's not sure. While eavesdropping earlier on Cara's conversation with Reed in her office, Nic overheard her suggesting it could be divinity or fate. Whether the connections are placed there by a supreme being, they're a metaphysical result, or just plain physics can be debated, but the threads do exist.

As Jake previously mentioned, if the general consensus is that we only use 10% of our brain, and if we do evolve, our brain should be able to harness more and more of its potential with each subsequent generation. On the physical plane, think of the powerful effect of social media and the way it has exploded exponentially across the globe. We are all linked, and only now with technology, we are starting to see that link.

Imagine with evolution, the powerful capability of the brain to move beyond the physical world. "Well, in our case we appear to have gone beyond the physical and even the metaphysical into telepathic, sharing our thoughts and spilling them into a cosmic consciousness."

Nic shakes his head slightly after his explanation to the group. It's humorous or eerily intentional that he knows so much on the topic. He acquired the knowledge well before he understood his own 'superpowers'.

His daughter's favorite programs to watch with him are *Ancient Aliens* and any show investigating unsolved phenomena. He's heard plenty of theorizing and debating about psychic abilities, shared consciousness, hive minds and the powerful capabilities of the human brain.

Furthermore, Cara's sister is a psychologist and a "New Age Guru" as Sasha refers to Danni. Danni has Cara's head filled with all the latest therapy techniques, meditation hints, and the power of sage. During the celebration of Beltane, or May Day as some may know it, Cara and Mia light a fire in the outdoor pit. They sing, dance and chant while they smudge the property with burnt sage. Mia really enjoys this bonding moment, so Nic has never bothered to investigate the why.

Besides, the why can be harmful to his mental health. Once, after an hour-long conversation on the phone with her sister, Cara hung up and stared at him for several uncomfortable minutes. When she finally spoke, she said, "I am trying to figure out what Love Language you are." This led to a debate on whether he was Touch and she was Words or vice versa. It ended in a stalemate, but they did both agree Sasha was Acts of Service. Nic has now learned not to pursue details on any of these topics unless he has the time and the interest. All in all, Danni's fascination with all of it is also eerily ironic.

Between aliens populating the earth thousands of years ago, all the psychobabble, and the Pagan rituals, he knows surprisingly more about the topic of collective consciousness than he would have guessed. Although, what he and his wife just achieved is beyond anything he can explain. It borders on the fantastical. Yet maybe it can be rationalized. Maybe they 'will' the talent into existence. Whatever the explanation, he senses they are only beginning to grasp the enormity of the gifts they may possess.

"But how was Sasha able to commandeer the steering of Cara's scan?" Jinx asks, still looking puzzled after his lengthy explanation and interrupting his thoughts.

Nic peers at his friend. "Ah, Sasha was different."

When Cara pulled his thread, not only did Sasha come into the pocket, but he was able to go beyond it; starting to travel on his own on the thread between Cara and himself. Sasha's mind can see the process and adapt.

"Like a computer worm or virus, Sasha can get in and decipher code and reroute or reprogram. He's a mind hacker," Jinx says by way of an explanation that makes sense to her computer engineering background.

"Nice description, Jinx. Makes me sound despicable," Sasha huffs.

"I think she's onto something, Sash. It could be the thing of beauty Jake describes when we're together. You are directing your gift and capitalizing my talent," Nic agrees.

Cara comes to Sasha's defense. "You are selling poor Broody short on this. There's more, but he's holding back. His mind and thread are different from yours, more dazzling and stouter. Remember the electrical charge we received when he attached himself to the group? He doesn't have a grid, but the grid may only be indicative of the photographic memory, not raw intelligence, or talent. When we tried to attach to Mia earlier, the charge she threw at us was very similar to the energy I felt from Sasha." Cara rests her eyes on Sasha with some scrutiny. "But yours was more subtle and controlled."

"Who was the guy we spotted?" Jinx adds.

Cara responds, "He's part of this, for sure. I received enough from him to know."

"Was it Ed?"

"No," Reed answers as he's coming down the stairs with a laptop in one hand and an IPad in the other. He hands the tablet to Sasha and the laptop to Nic informing them he has the results from the search of Ed's apartment and his records from prison. He has the Wi-Fi password but to plug in the printer password in case they want a paper copy for everyone to review.

Cara goes off topic while they are reviewing the search results, "I feel the overwhelming need to cook." She lifts a chin to her boyfriend. "Reed, how about you and I head to that fine grocery store I was telling you about?"

From the look on Reed's face, Nic isn't the only one reading Cara's thoughts. Reed tips his chin back at Cara. "On the way to the store, I want to hit the spot mystery man was parked. He is long gone, but there might be some residual haze left behind that we can work with."

Cara points to him, Sasha, and Jake, barking her own orders, "You guys can play with Reed's new intel," before adding in a sweeter tone, "and please check on the kids. Make sure they're not driving poor Carter crazy."

"Vizzini, I don't think it's wise for you to go out right now," Sasha comments with concern.

No one has noticed, but when Cara returned from the bedroom, she was wearing a light jacket. She swings the jacket open on the left to reveal she's holstered with the Glock, having lifted her favorite weapon back from Reed, earlier. "Besides, have you already forgotten I can read minds? I can identify mystery man's thread now. And we can take Far Guard and post him outside." She looks to Jinx. "Wanna come?"

Jinx gives Cara her 'are you joking' face. "No way I'm missing all the fun when the ladies of this community see us with a fourth hot guy at the store." Jinx jumps up, grabbing Cara's arm. "Promise you'll throw me their thoughts when they see us with Reed, please?"

Cara giggles while pulling out an Indians baseball cap from her jacket pocket and handing it to Reed. "Take off that ridiculous blue blazer and put this hat on."

She gives him one of Sasha's leather jackets on the way out. "On the rare chance someone actually watches CNN in this town, you should be unrecognizable."

CHAPTER 7

"WE'RE BACK!" CARA ANNOUNCES, BUT no one is in the kitchen. She heaves her grocery bags onto the counter with Jinx and Reed following suit. Cara immediately starts pulling out pots and pans and ingredients to make her mother's Sicilian meat sauce, sugo.

Reed is watching his girlfriend, carefully. Their little trip to buy groceries was quite the experience. Successful, yet heartbreaking. While Cara was able to throw thoughts to Jinx in the store, she sent all the emotions to him. It was truly horrid. Jinx finally had to stop Cara. She was in tears over the mental insults being hurled at them. Vicious soccer moms judging Jinx and Cara's appearance and wondering how they so undeservedly got their claws into such astonishingly handsome husbands. Even their children were commented on. No vile stone was left unturned. And the emotional lashing...it was a crash course on the seven deadly sins. It was unbearable. No wonder Cara has always been so humble when it comes to her looks. As strong as she appears on the outside, she's obviously vulnerable to the chatter that has been attacking her subconscious.

Reed can't get the nastiness out of his head. Looking at Cara now, she seems composed, but those words and emotions likely caused some damage. Or maybe, they didn't. Maybe she's lived with the criticism so long, she has adapted. Judging from her focus on making the sauce though, he can tell she is affected. She has always told him that women are their own worst enemies. He never understood until now.

Men don't evaluate each other with the same kind of venom. They can't be bothered with any of that. But women...are vipers. He understands the "boys club" and "glass ceiling" issues that have existed. That's enough for women to have to deal with. But he believes women are the far stronger sex and has often wondered why more haven't progressed further in industry and politics. In the last 70 years, women have just begun to make a dent in the overall one percent. But who can achieve success with that kind of scrutiny and self-flagellation?

Cara always said she could never work for a woman because women don't have each other's backs. Women cannot see each other as anything but competition in the business world. They will use sex as a tool and pit men against each other, but they will not allow another woman onto their playing field. She used to joke about it being some dormant genetic code from the past to be the last woman standing in the field. Let all the cavemen fight over her. After hearing the backbiting and cruel contempt from those fake-tanned, Botoxed, dimwitted housewives at the grocery store, he must agree.

Wait, did he just judge those women? Holy shit, he's becoming a woman himself from all this oversharing with his girlfriend. Doing the only thing he can think of, he pulls Cara to his chest for a long, solid hug. Without thinking about it, he pulls Jinx into the hug as well.

Bringing their heads to his mouth, he whispers, "I know I didn't tell you both enough how proud I am of you. Not only are both of you gorgeous on the outside, but brilliant and kind and caring on the inside. Even more, you both have a set of brass balls most men would envy. I love you guys."

Jinx punches him in the abs. "Stop that, Reed! You are going to make me cry again today."

His girl kisses the spot Jinx hit, and then wraps her arms more tightly around him.

Most of the prep work is done when the other three men make their way into the kitchen. Reed is rolling out meatballs as Jinx washes the dishes and cleans up the cooking mess. Cara stirs, adding some final spices. Short of Reed's emotional moment, they have kept conversation to a minimum during the preparation. Both Jinx and Reed know Cara requires mental solitude on occasion and this looked to be one of those.

Cooking for her is an outlet. She will take on tasks like cooking or cleaning, hyperfocusing on the exercise, essentially emptying her mind of any other thoughts. Reed keeps watching her from the corner of his eyes. This realization does reconcile all the, sometimes, odd behavior she's exhibited in the past. Although, when her need to cook and clean happened at Reed's place, he couldn't be happier or more encouraging of her oddness.

With his eyes still on her, she finally turns to give Reed her full attention. It's apparent he is highly disturbed by what happened at the grocery store. He need not worry. Cara has already disassociated, or compartmentalized, or whatever psych term is correct.

"I thought I was the Meatball Making King of this house," Sasha declares, offended, and interrupting everyone's deep thoughts when he suddenly appears in the kitchen.

"No, I'm the Meatball Making Queen, and Reed is a fine Roller. He has held that position far longer than you, Sasha," Cara quips back.

Nic questions this as he's waltzing in. "You make sugo with Reed?"

Cara glares at her husband. "Nic, I've been making sugo for Reed since the 80's. I still make it for him when I visit. It's tomato sauce, not children. Where were you guys?"

Nic is watching Reed roll out the final meatballs while he responds, "We were down in my office using the work boards to create a flow chart of facts on all this new intel. Did you guys get anything from the theater parking lot?"

"Not really. A few little things I've stored. You ready to mind palace, or do I need to see your flow chart first?" The little mental game they have always played together as a couple to sort out their issues received a name a few days ago. The BBC's *Sherlock* series gets the credit.

"Skip the chart, it may hamper rather than help."

"K," Cara says without looking at him. She needs twenty minutes to finish, wash up and core dump the intrusive thoughts from earlier. Forget disassociating, she wants them erased.

They relocate to the living room and everyone sits down comfortably, except Cara, who remains standing. Jinx has a pen and paper. Reed has his tablet poised and Sasha is sitting between them. Jake is seated next to Nic, ready to assist if necessary.

"You ready?" Nic asks his wife.

Cara starts to pace. She has a bad feeling this exercise is going to prove difficult. "Nic, let's start with the actual man in the Camry. Middle aged, foreign, been here in the states for a while."

"Incarcerated," Nic adds.

Cara nods her affirmation. "That's the connection to Ed, same prison. But who is he?"

"Connection to a third interested party," Nic blurts out.

"Yes, but let's focus on one person at a time."

She asks Nic to scan through and find Camry guy's memories of Ed and feed them to her. Cara can see Reed tapping away at his tablet, probably requesting inmate and release records.

"He didn't know Ed previously and didn't like him when they first met, but somehow, they find a connection and become friends...or is it partners with a common enemy?" Nic asks.

Cara is still pacing, but she likes the direction they're going in. "Partners. I like partners. Commonality?"

Nic's eyes are moving back and forth quickly. "Pictures. I see pictures, moving pictures. Recent but also, maybe a year or 18 months ago."

"Yes, that's when they make the connection. It's a video. Leave it for now, Nic. Zero in on his memories of Ed. Besides the obvious motive, what else are you getting? Why the kids? Why are we feeling the kids with him?"

"He hates the kids. No, not hates, fears. He fears the kids. It starts with you, though. You, and the kids by extension. Why fear?"

"Ed has his own talents and he is using them now. We need an inventory of his gifts. What can he do? Can you see his talent in the memory?" She needs to get to the bottom of why her children feel like the real target.

Nic places his fingers to his temples. "I can't see past..."

Cara comes around, closer, and stops behind her husband. "It must be done, Nic," she says very calmly, and places her hand on the back of his neck.

"Baby, he may know."

"What does it matter? He already knows more about us than we know about him. We must, Nic, it's the only way." Without some solid clues, they will never figure this out.

"What are you going to do?" Sasha asks, interrupting them.

They are going to follow the threads after all. The thread mystery, middle-aged, foreign man has to Ed. The second thread, a memory from what Nic seized during the smash and grab, and the third thread, the connection from Cara to mystery man.

"Won't mystery man know you've come knocking?" Sasha questions, concerned.

The best defense is a good offense. It's time to take down the door and storm the castle. Camry man knows where they are, and he knows of Cara's abilities. They are at a disadvantage by not going in. If they can determine his motive and true capabilities, it will move the advantage back to their team.

Nic places his hand over Cara's on his neck. They both shut their eyes and their heads tilt in unison. Motionless, even their breathing seems to slow. Suddenly, Nic's eyes pop back open, again in unison with Cara's. Nic removes his hand from Cara's and places it back on his lap. They are in a trancelike state for a few minutes. No one in the room dares utter a sound. Slowly, Cara comes out of the trance and moves her hand away from Nic's neck. She thoughtfully shifts around him so she's standing in front of him, all while looking at his face.

When Nic finally looks up at her, he states with no inflection, "You are his Voldemort."

"Who?!" Reed yells out.

Cara turns to him. "He Who Must Not Be Named," she says, still in deep thought.

"What the hell are you talking about?" Reed asks, losing his patience. This causes Cara to snap out of her thoughts.

"Jesus, Reed, you really need to start reading fiction more, or reading People magazine or something. Now, that we don't hang out on a regular basis, your knowledge of contemporary pop culture is severely lacking," Cara quips.

Sasha tries to quell the tension. "Reed, I think Ed thinks he's the 'Boy Who Lived'. He thinks he's Harry Potter. He believes Cara is his Voldemort. One must die for the other to live."

Cara manages a small smile for Sasha. "Mia would be very proud of you, Sasha."

"How many frigging times have I had to watch those movies with her? I can quote them for God's sake. So, what are you saying, Ed's become delusional?"

Nic jumps in explaining that Ed's talents mimic Cara's. He is a telepath and an empath. "He thinks he was spared for a reason in the confrontation with her years ago. Ed became obsessed with the Harry Potter books in prison and related everything about Harry to his own life and his gifts. Ed believes he's the 'Boy Who Lived.' In his mind, Cara became the evil Voldemort. He thought she was dead until he met the Camry man in prison. The information the man provided lets Ed know for certain that his Voldemort truly lives. And just like in the books, only one of them can survive."

"He's insane, we knew THAT from the beginning," Cara exclaims. She suddenly turns to Reed, seething, "You should have let me cut off his nuts like I wanted to. He would have bled to death, and Voldemort would live. The maniacal villain wins this tale."

Nic stands and grabs his wife's wrist, firmly. "That's it, Cara! That's the thread between you. You WERE supposed to kill him 25 years ago!"

Reed whispers quietly, "Or he was supposed to kill her. The thread had to be cut, but it wasn't."

The room is silent once again. Jinx is still writing on the pad, but Cara can't imagine what the words are.

It's Sasha who breaks the silence. "What's with the kids? Why hunt them?"

Nic mumbles, "He sees them as an extension of Cara. Evil minions, Death Eater spawn, so to speak."

"Okay, this is bad, but it's good we know. We can factor in 'fucking crazy' on your flow chart and move on. At least my life is starting to elevate from B movie status," Cara adds to lighten the mood.

"So, back to the middleman," Nic says dismissively, walking back to his chair.

"Nic! That's what he is, a middleman." Inspiration hits her hard.

Camry man has no connection to Cara. He's an intermediary between Ed and another interested party. The connection was random. Serendipitous. The middleman doesn't have any motive of his own. He's tied to someone else, aside from Ed. They must follow middleman's thread out to that second party, the interested party, to discern their motive. It must be the person or group that funded the hit from Vlad and wants the kids.

"Wait, Ed is after Cara Bianco, but is this second interested party after Chase Bennett?" Reed asks trying to follow this mind palace routine they are doing with each other. It's obvious he's very disturbed she has yet another adversary he's failed to protect her from.

Nic and Cara give each other the look, again, the one nobody in the room seems to understand. Nic reaches his hand out to her. While Cara places her hand in his, Nic says a little too calmly in response to the question, "No. This second party has no prior connection to Cara, at all. The other person or group…is connected to me."

Sasha jumps out of his chair, gesturing at Nic. "You mean to tell me that Ed is looking to kill Cara and her kids, and then he runs into someone in prison who knows of a second party also looking to kill Cara and her kids - but because of something you've done, Nic?"

"Yes…sort of," Nic admits, reluctantly.

Jake who has remained quiet and alert during the whole mind palace act finally decides to comment. "Don't get me wrong; I am thoroughly impressed today with what you two have done with this breakthrough. It's fucking remarkable. But why is it so hard to get intel on the second party when you had so much on Ed?"

When Nic did the grab, he went looking for memories of Ed because he knew Ed was involved. Only having seconds to find relevant memories, he focused where it made sense. The other memories had some heavy blocks on them. Nic didn't bother to dig. The time would have been wasted. Those blocked memories were peripheral at that point. There, but slightly out of his reach.

Middleman was mostly blocked like everyone else in the house is. Cara did receive some emotions from him but no thoughts. She recommends they make another mind palace attempt combining Nic's fringe memories and the emotions she came away with.

It was a set up, you know, Cara transmits to her husband.

Yes, the middleman wanted us to see Ed memories. He covered the 2nd party. He's connected more intimately with that other party. I believe they were going to let Ed take the fall for the murders. This was planned.

I agree, but let's think about this. I get the feeling we need to proceed with caution. Why do I feel that way? Like I'm about to walk out onto a minefield.

I'm sensing that, too.

"Wait." Jake states. "Isn't it too coincidental that you're given free passage to the Ed memories, but the other party and their motive is blocked from you? It sounds like a set up. This middleman has talent. He came here specifically to lead us to Ed, thus concealing the greater threat, the second party."

Damn that Jack Reacher.

"You already figured this out, didn't you?" Jake accuses.

"You read minds now?" Nic inquires with some attitude.

"No. It's written all over you. Nice poker faces, guys. Were you not going to share that?"

"Yes, we were, but we're still processing. Don't get your panties in a bunch, JACK," Cara retorts. This produces a menacing growl from Jake, but Cara catches an emotion from Reed at her comment...*What is it?*

Satisfaction, is Nic's telepathic response.

Shit, I forgot you were in here! Sorry, babe. Welcome to my world of talking to myself!

This does take some getting used to, huh?

They both begin laughing, appearing insane. Noticing the others staring, they shake their heads trying to regain composure. Neither feels an explanation is necessary. Releasing Cara's hand, Nic sits back in his chair. "Round Two in the mind palace."

Cara, again, begins to pace around the room. She is visibly squinting her eyes this time as she walks. There is tremendous emotion around the second party. Whereas Ed is delusional, this person or group is all regret, rage, and revenge. It's different though; somehow inconsistent. "I feel it through the middleman but it's not..."

"It's not the same level of emotion," Nic adds. He can feel the difference, too. He doesn't recognize what it is, but it feels like one person, not a group.

Cara has moved to pacing a smaller portion of the living room, directly in front of everyone seated there. Her fingertips rub her temples while she paces. The afternoon's mental activities are taking a toll. After two full rounds of pacing with no one speaking, Cara stops in front of Nic and looks at him. She turns abruptly to gawk at Jinx, and it hits her. A straight punch to her gut from the memory of the grocery store gossip.

Jinx looks up defensively. "What?"

"OH MY GOD, NIC!" Cara exclaims. "We don't recognize the emotion because we're looking at it all wrong. It's FEMININE!"

Nic reexamines the processes in his mind and his face registers the result. "The second party is a woman!"

Cara begins to scowl and leans in to place her hands on Nic's chair. She gets right in his face. Her eyes become hard, and she speaks clearly, positive she recognizes the emotion now. "Not just any woman, Nic. The Hell hath no fury like a woman scorned kind of woman! Care to elaborate?!" Nic's face falls flat while Cara's turns to seething, jealous fury. "What haven't you shared with me, my love?!"

CHAPTER 8

THE VISIBLE FURY EMANATING FROM Cara is making the group uncomfortable. Nic is lost, not being able to reconcile what his brain is receiving from Cara with what's being processed in there.

No, you're jumping to conclusions here. You're correct, she is a woman scorned, but it can't be me, Cara. I told you I've never been in a relationship. I didn't lie to you. Yes, there were women, but none I saw more than a couple of times.

How about during ops? Seductions? Cara drills.

No, that wasn't my area of expertise. I told you already.

Nic, with your looks, you're telling me you didn't seduce women as part of your work?

Sure, I flirted and 'preened' as you refer to it, but no, bedding them was not my specialty. I...would've had some issues with that.

What are you talking about, issues? You're like a sex machine! You're amazing in bed. I thought you were a total player after our first night.

Player?! You need to calm down, Cara, and trust me. It was all about you on our first night. I've never had anything like that happen to me. I'll send you my memory of it...later. Although, I sort of like this crazy, jealous bitch thing you have going on. I must admit, it's very reaffirming.

You trying to defuse the situation?

YES, you're going postal on me and I'm losing focus. SO. ARE. YOU.

Fine, you're right, I'm calming down. I do want that memory later, though. I shared mine with you, earlier.

Which, by the way, was very emotive. I had no idea you felt that way the morning after our first night together. AND YET, you still question me?

I trust you. I do. But are you sure there isn't some crazy bunny boiler you slept with once who's out there trying to kill me and our kids? Because that IS what we're feeling on this. Clearly.

But it doesn't make sense.

They need to reexamine the connection to him. It isn't clear. Her motive is, her targets are, but the connection is hazy. There is some deep emotion there. This isn't a one-night stand gone stalker. This is a woman who has some time invested, who is avenging a deep, deep betrayal.

Cara leans away from Nic and composes her face. She turns and sees everyone watching in curious horror. She doesn't think she can continue to mind palace this out loud to the group anymore. Reed, feeling her distress, is on the edge of his seat, the Captain, ready to pounce. She's not getting rid of either of them easily. She sends a message to Jinx.

"Jake, let's get dinner started. The sauce should be ready. You set the table and I'll make the penne…and Cara, thank you for asking instead of just throwing the suggestion at me." Jinx gives her a smirk and a wink as she drags her husband out of the living room.

Cara reciprocates with an appreciative smile. She looks to Reed wanting to try something. She can see her own concern on his face and feels his alarm coming back at her.

Connor? It's fine…I'm okay…I just had an overreaction. Nic and I would be more comfortable without so many people in attendance for the rest of this. Do you hear me?

Cara is only watching Reed from the corner of her eye. She sees him tilt his head and wipe his face with his hands. Then, a slow, subtle nod comes from him.

We would like you and Sasha to stay, but if this gets too emotional, I'm going to ask you to grab Sasha and get out, as well. Capice?

Reed moves his head towards the kitchen and touches his ear, their signal for 'all set'.

Nic interrupts, *You and I are soooo having a little 'talk' tonight, cara mia.*

Duly noted, once again. Let's proceed. As painful as this woman's betrayal is, you know we need to get inside of it to find the answer. Her emotion is the only thing we have at this point to go on.

Nic stands, wanting to stretch, and knowing this isn't going to be easy.

Reed and Sasha watch as Cara and Nic get up and move towards the center of the room, closer to where they're seated. They clasp hands, more from the need to touch than the need for connection.

Ready? Cara nods.

OH GOD Nic, it's awful…the pain…it's everywhere. Cara leans forward to clasp her abdomen from the physical pain. Even Nic is hunching towards her, his face flinching.

She was hurt, wounded physically and emotionally by this man. She's never recovered. He has ruined her life. His death isn't enough. She needs him suffering…emotionally devastated as her revenge. Nic gets this out. She can hear the pain in his mental voice.

She doesn't want to hurt him, physically. She doesn't want to KILL him. Just annihilate him emotionally…she still loves him. She knows the way to do that is through me and the kids.

Yes, she keeps something of him…Cara, what is it she keeps…a memory? No…something more tangible.

Yes…she always keeps it on her. Like a talisman.

However painful, Cara, the talisman is the key. Please, try and see it.

Cara takes a deep breath. The pain is so intense. Pain like she has never experienced before, deep, wrenching, and anguished. It makes her shudder, tears bursting from her eyes. The emotions twist with desperation and rage. Nic releases her hands to pull her closer. His face etched with torment.

Even in her mind Cara can barely give Nic the words…*Erghh, it's…a picture of them. She keeps…keeps…a photo.*

Baby, focus. Please focus on the photo. Can you make out faces?

OOOHHH Nic, it hurts so much!

Cara's practically convulsing, shaking so hard. Nic tightens his grip around her. The photo begins to materialize in their minds. First the woman, she is young, vibrant, and very beautiful. She has a cascading flow of copper hair. She is smiling like she has everything in the world to live for, a woman madly in love.

Nic jerks back slightly at the sight of the woman. *Baby? I've never in my life seen this woman before, and please remember I have a photographic memory. I'm sorry, but you need to expand the picture and see the rest of it.*

Cara moans as she continues her assault on the pain-stricken emotions. The only thing holding her upright at this point is Nic. And suddenly the photo expands. It's an old school selfie. Shot with an instamatic type of camera. The man is clearer. He's young, and he's smiling that same wide grin as the woman. He has dark, slightly disheveled wavy hair. He could be standing in the wind, or just had it tousled. He is strikingly handsome.

Nic immediately drops his arms and steps away from Cara, causing her to go crashing to the carpet. She is outright sobbing. Reed lurches for her and scoops her up onto his lap in one fluid movement. He begins rocking her and wiping her tears. Sasha moves with the same grace to Nic's side full of concern. The handlers appear as if they are taking sides in a marital battle.

Nic is immobile. His face has transformed. Evil Nic. Deadly steel eyes.

Reed's entire focus is on Cara. She is a mess, inconsolable and emotionally anguished. He's clutching her to his chest, hoping he can send her this comfort energy they say he can emit. He finally lifts his eyes to Nic. Her husband is just standing there, his arms at his sides. His fists are clenched, and he is emanating pure furious wrath. Reed's mouth drops open because he can feel it. He looks quickly to Sasha and notices the man registering Nic's anger, leaning away from him.

"Cara, you know what must be done," is all Nic says.

She can't even verbalize, mentally, but nods to her husband while she roughly removes Reed's arms from around her.

Nic is a blur. He steps behind Sasha while Cara jumps up into Nic arms, essentially wedging Sasha between them. The reaction is instantaneous. Sasha groans while thrashing, not in an effort to hurt them, but from the violent assault they have perpetrated on his mind. Sasha continues to moan from the intrusion, and then from the memory as Nic and Cara wrench it from him with no thought of sparing him the rape.

When Nic releases his arms, Cara stumbles back away from Sasha. Reed catches her before she falls. He's completely clueless and growing more alarmed while he clutches her back to his chest. Why did they do that to Sasha?

Dropping down to his knees, Sasha's head falls forward and it hits the carpet. He looks like he's praying except his body is trembling. Still standing, with his head inclined and staring at the only person he called family until he met Cara, is Nic. His face is a mask showing no emotion. He really is one scary son of a bitch.

CHAPTER 9

REED, TAKE ME TO THE family room and grab Jinx and Jake along the way, please.

Reed pulls Cara up into his arms and carries her out. Cara is crying harder than before. As they pass the kitchen, Reed motions for Jinx and Jake while they continue through the kitchen to the smaller, more intimate and casual family room on the other side.

On their way in, Jinx flips the switch to turn on the gas fireplace in the room. Reed sits on the stone hearth with a sobbing Cara still held tightly in his arms. He doesn't know what to do to calm her down. He's wiping tears and rocking her, rubbing her back and stroking her hair. But she knows none of Reed's efforts are going to shake what she and Nic pulled from Sasha.

Then Cara starts to hear it…in her head. The music…she knows it… it's the strums of a bass guitar from one of the songs she hears late at night coming from the music room…maybe October Project? Then comes the voice, shaky, anguished, and tormented, singing about haunted dreams and being caged, the past never leaving his mind, and a funeral in his heart. It's not Nic's voice, though. It's Sasha singing. *Please Nic, disconnect. I can't take it right now,* Cara pleads mentally.

After Nic vacates abruptly, Cara realizes she's not alone. Reed. She kept his thread pulled in her mind. She looks up at him and his eyes are red rimmed and glassy. He's just experienced all of that with her. She places her hand up to his face and leans in for their foreheads to touch. *I'm sorry, I didn't mean to have you feel that awful anguish, first hers, then his. I'll be ok. I just need to let the emotions pass. It's crazy, isn't it? I've cried more in the last 72 hours than I have my whole life.* Cara releases Reed's connection and attempts to process all this chaos and try for some semblance of composure.

When she can finally have a clear thought, she reaches her hand out to Jake. He doesn't hesitate and clasps it with both of his, engulfing her small one inside his very large paws. He nods to her in understanding. His face suddenly changes; he inhales a hard, shaky breath, and drops to one knee, involuntarily.

Cara gives him a moment to process what she sent him. When he looks back up at her, showing the most emotion she has ever seen on his face, Jake utters the only words he can form, "Holy. Shit."

"Yes," Cara confirms.

With her voice still shaky, she makes some requests. It's a music video the ginger made the connection with. It's something the kids posted online, probably YouTube. Cara wants Jake to grab the kids downstairs and use Nic's office to have them pull up all the videos of their open mic night performances, and the ones they film in the music room. Find any that have Sasha in them. Nic and Sasha have a rule. They don't let the kids post the ones they appear in, but somehow one or two have made their way to the Internet. They must find them.

"Delete all the videos, regardless of my children's protests, but download a copy of any you find with Nic or Sasha in them, first." They need to watch those. While Jake is doing that, she is going to endeavor to explain to Jinx and Reed what has just transpired. Her final request is he leave Sasha and Nic alone on his way by.

Cara turns her face back to Reed. "Do you know who Katherine St. John is?"

"I know of the Katherine St. John who's the daughter of the former MI6 serving Chief, Thomas St. John," Reed acknowledges.

As Jake quickly passes by the living room, Nic catches a glimpse of him in his peripheral vision. Nic is staring down at Sasha who is still on the floor. All he can think is, this is a fucking mess. Nic's rage has subsided and he's left with nothing but emptiness and the sound of Sasha's tormented singing in his head. The lyrics tell of a person who has lost himself and is alone in his life. It's seriously depressing. As he listens to Broody, Nic can't prevent the tiny smile on his lips when he thinks of his wife's accurate description of him and Sasha with their dark, moody, and broody personalities. He hates when she's right.

Not knowing what he should do, Nic gets down on the floor next to Sasha, sitting tailor style. He listens to Sasha hit the chorus with haunting echoes, but otherwise he just sits.

Um, Cara? I know I'm not supposed to bother you but, um, I'm at a bit of a loss here. Comforting middle-aged anguished men is not my area of expertise. This is sort of your domain, no? I mean you are Italian, and melodrama and tragedy are in your DNA.

What. The. Fuck? You are the man with the ANGST! Suck on that for some inspiration! For God's sake, put on your big boy underpants, place your hand on his shoulder and ask him to start telling you the story, from the beginning. I'm finishing the wrap up in here. I want to start Reed and Jinx on some research and data collection. Oh, and I've sent Jake to look at videos to find the point of origin. And Nic?

Yes?

You're starting to appear as the weak link in our partnership.

I'm starting to believe I am, cara mia.

I'll be in there as soon as I'm done here. Get him to talk, please.

Nic follows his orders and reaches out to Sasha, placing his hand tentatively on his shoulder. He gently asks Sasha to tell him what happened. He even throws in a couple of 'pleases'. Sasha doesn't acknowledge him, though. Nic tries to do that energy thing Jake was talking about where he can send comfort and warmth through his touch. He isn't sure if he's done it correctly until Sasha finally looks up at him.

"Are you trying to comfort me?" Nic nods. "DO NOT EXTEND ME ANY COMFORT," Sasha says articulating each word. "I don't deserve that."

"Sash, story, from the beginning, NOW!" Nic barks, deciding more force is required.

Instead of talking, Sasha sings another verse of the song aloud, but softly, as he pulls his head from the floor and leans back, slouched against the front of a plush chair with his legs spread.

Then, abruptly, Sasha just stops singing and looks to Nic, feeling resigned. "Just after you got settled at your new job, I was sent away for nine months on assignment." Nic nods at the recollection. "I was only 20 years old...I was sent under deep cover to infiltrate England's Military Intelligence, Section 6."

He was supposed to use his high marks in Whore School, as well as his exemplary training, to seduce, bed, and eventually get engaged to Katherine St. John, the daughter of the then Assistant Chief at MI6, Thomas St. John.

Sasha was a young man. He didn't really understand what was involved. Even if he had, Sasha would not have been able to deny the order. He was given a new cover as a student at Cambridge, where Katherine was attending. He was supposed to be the son of West German, wealthy parents, but most of his academic life was spent in Great Britain at various schools. Someone, already inside, on a lower level, had paved the way for Sasha by forging documents at all the proper primary schools in England. He was to sound like a Brit, but with a slight German accent. That was the only easy part of the assignment.

Sasha arrived at Cambridge looking and dressing the part. He was matched into three of her classes. Katherine was only 18 years old. She was far more beautiful than he thought she would be. He took his time trying to get to know her, and then courting her. He utilized the sum of his education. That's all he had, what he had studied. Sasha hadn't really dated or spent any time with women. They didn't have those kinds of opportunities in training.

He looks to Nic waiting for some acknowledgement, and when Nic nods, Sasha continues.

He found he enjoyed her company. She was very bright. She loved life and appreciated all its nuances. She relished life's simple pleasures. Katherine wasn't what Sasha expected from a girl raised in a privileged environment. It took him by surprise if he's being honest.

Sasha pauses for a moment to reflect. His brain feels melted from both the rape and the memory.

He tried to match all his interests with Katherine's. Nineteenth century Romanticism was her specialty, so it became his. They would read Byron and Shelly under a tree together and go for long walks to discuss the literature. Sasha was enjoying it.

Katherine wasn't the type of girl who savored crowds or attention. Their occasional trips to pubs and parties in the academic environment were something Sasha had never experienced and he found them entertaining. But she was more content with her solitary time spent with him.

The weeks turned to three months and Katherine finally asked him to meet her parents. They went into London and met with her folks at their flat for dinner. Her father seemed tentative, but cordial. Sasha was pleased, as he still saw the meeting as progress.

During this time, he tried to keep their physical relationship to stolen kisses and light contact. Sasha attempted to follow the books Katherine was so fond of, becoming the courteous, romantic hero. He never pushed for more than that.

The University was going into break for the holidays and he was invited to spend New Year's with her in London. Again, he saw Katherine's father who was beginning to show more kindness, even complimenting Sasha on his care of Katherine. The man commented he had never seen her happier. Sasha was getting more excited by his progress.

When they got back to the routine at school, Katherine began to press the physical part of their relationship. She wanted more. He had to give in at some point, so Sasha let her set the pace. He thought it prudent.

Sasha lets out a big sigh. "We progressed on that front quickly to an all-out sexual relationship. She was very prolific, and, I was afraid, beginning to fall in love with me."

"Did you love her?" Cara asks very softly as she comes in behind Sasha and sits next to him on the floor.

Sasha winces slightly before answering, "I don't know. I wasn't an experienced man. I was never loved and I don't think I knew what love was at that point. I knew training and duty. My only bond of affection was what I had for Nic. But I knew enough to realize what she was feeling for me. Still, I had my mission." Sasha inhales deeply before continuing.

Their relationship progressed hot and heavy until spring when he was sent orders to propose. Sasha discerned the timing was quick. They were both still so young, but his superiors were thrilled with his progress and wanted him poised to infiltrate the family.

Sasha took the opportunity on their next visit with her family to speak to her father, alone. He explained his feelings for Katherine and that he wanted to ask for her hand, promising not to marry until they were older and out of school, but explaining he wanted to commit to her and only her. Her father didn't object. Consequently, he planned a very romantic moment and asked her to marry him.

"Of course, she was thrilled." Sasha has his head in his hands, barely capable of talking.

They were engaged for eight weeks when it happened. They went for a walk in the woods to discuss books and admire nature. When they returned to her flat, she opened the door to find her father and two of his agents pointing pistols.

Sasha is beginning to lose it again. Tears are running down his face. He is not sure he can continue. "I don't know what happened to me, but in that instant, nothing was in my head but my training...nothing." He takes some quick, shaky breaths just to resume.

He placed Katherine in front of him. He knew he was the target. He knew that somehow his cover was blown, so he used her as a shield. Her father was screaming at him to let her go, but he couldn't. He wouldn't. He backed them up to the doorway. He was going to drag her through then run, but that's not what happened.

Very gently Nic coaxes Sasha on, "What happened, Sash?"

The two agents panicked. They aimed their weapons at any exposed part of Sasha's body, hoping to get a shot off before he got past the doorway, but he kept Katherine perfectly in front of him until the door. At the door, he was going to push her back into the room, but the exact moment he propelled her forward, one of the agents fired at his leg. Katherine was already in motion. The bullet hit her in the abdomen.

"I didn't stay to see her fall to the ground. I was around the corner, out the door, in the cover of shadows, and on my way to a safe house before I even heard the ambulance." Sasha gets the last part out quickly. He can't tolerate speaking the words that changed his life.

Nic looks to his wife before refocusing on Sasha who is wiped out. His head is down, his body slouched. He just can't continue, but he knows they need more.

CHAPTER 10

CARA KNOWS HER HUSBAND IS useless right now. It's up to her. She cajoles Sasha into continuing. "Katherine survived the shooting. She lived, but the damage to her reproductive organs…they couldn't be salvaged. Katherine became unstable when she was told who you really were, Sash. Between the shooting, the loss of her fertility, and the betrayal, she had a breakdown. Her father institutionalized her. She spent the next 15 years in an asylum. You tortured yourself and kept track of her, didn't you? DIDN'T YOU?" Cara shouts.

"YES, YES, I did! How could I…" Sasha just dissolves.

Nic is up and out of the room, heading to find Reed to see what he's gathered on intel. He can't bear the sight of his 'brother' falling apart. *Sorry, baby, but you really are better with the Angst.*

Cara tries to gather Sasha in her arms as best she can and holds him. She strains desperately to tone down the tremendous guilt flooding her from his emotions. *Max? Can you and your sister come upstairs and show your Uncle Sasha how much you love him, please.*

We're feeling his distress, Mom. Mia gathered the story, as well.

Then you understand what I need you to do.

Cara is still holding Sasha when she can hear the kids on the stairs. She quickly wipes away his tears and tucks his hair behind his ears. She stands, leaving a spot on each side of Sasha open for them. They plop down and do what children all over the world can do with a just a smile. They mend his tortured heart.

Mia hugs him hard, whispering her love and praises, giving him encouragement. Max only cuddles with Sasha, something they've always done together. Max was the more physically affectionate of the two kids and Sasha the recipient of most of his attention. He also whispers kind words of love and his reassurance, reminding Sasha how much he has meant to them, even conceding Sasha has done more for them than either parent.

Cara stands back and watches her children interact with Sasha, struck by their love for him and his for them. She is so proud of her children right at that moment. But the moment passes and her lips frown. The frown is slowly replaced with a look of calm. The calm, still transforming her face, and hardening her features. Her eyes turn cold and dark. Her jaw becomes set and her lips thin. A look of steely determination takes over.

The twins are still gathered in Sasha arms when Nic and Reed approach the living room. Taking note of Cara's expression, Reed stops Nic in the archway. "Look at your wife's face." Nic stares at Cara and turns back to Reed with questioning eyes. "You don't see that look often, I imagine. I haven't seen it in quite some time. That's her mission set face. Best we hang back and watch from a safe distance."

Cara looks down at her children and informs them it's time to get ready for dinner. "Head upstairs to your rooms and wash up. Be back in 20 minutes, please."

The twins register her steely mood and rise quickly to exit, passing Nic and Reed on their way out of the room.

When Cara knows they are far enough away, she says, "Sasha, please stand up."

Sasha is hesitant, but he stands facing Cara. She winds up and slaps him across the face with as much brute force as she can manage. While he's still registering the shock from her assault, Cara shoves him hard, sending him backwards to land seated in the plush chair.

She gets right into his face and starts screaming, "You need to snap out of it, now! You need to get over this guilt for hurting her NOW! And do you know why, Sasha, DO YOU? BECAUSE I WILL FIND KATHERINE AND KILL HER!!!"

Sicilian Personality Disorder has set in, firmly. Cara has had some success learning to control the overwhelming fury that can ignite her into an insane rage. Over the years, Reed has helped her figure out when to use it to her advantage and when to hold back. It's an interesting phenomenon and her family jokes about it so often, it has received its own name and acronym, SPD. They all have it. She has an entire extended family of crazy hotheads. Unleashing her inner SPD in certain situations can provoke a positive result. Cara has obviously concluded this is one of those moments.

Sasha's eyes grow wide as Cara continues her full-on offensive. "NO ONE THREATENS ME OR MY CHILDREN AND LIVES, SASHA. I DON'T GIVE A RAT'S ASS ABOUT YOUR GUILT OR YOUR ANGST! YOU WERE DOING YOUR JOB, SOLDIER! ANY ONE OF US WOULD HAVE DONE THE SAME THING!"

Nic looks to Reed, and they both say simultaneously, "The Italian Love Treatment."

Reed starts to chuckle, but Nic adds, "The guy's a fucking mess. I hope it works."

Cara grabs Sasha by his shirt pulling him even closer to her face. She looks like the quintessential drill Sargent at Army basic. The look on her face, her body language and emotional onslaught, are nothing short of terrifying.

"You must get a handle on this, Sasha. You've carried it too far. She was not the love of your life, and I understand she was collateral damage, but SHIT HAPPENS! It sucks, but you compartmentalize and move on. WHAT THE FUCK?! Did they not teach that in your training?!"

Sasha finally gets the nerve to respond to her, "What do you know of this? YOU, who were raised in a loving home."

Cara turns away from him to try for some composure, but she fails, turning back and hitting him hard in the chest. "That's exactly where you learn it, dumb ass!"

Reed can't prevent the smile forming on his lips. Of course, Cara is correct. Compartmentalizing is a learned behavior everyone acquires in a loving home. If you have a brother or sister, you learn to tuck away your anger and disappointment. Some siblings thrive on ratting each other out to their parents or accusing them by telling wicked lies. Some steal favorite clothes and ruin them. They destroy perfect Friday nights out with friends by getting a parent to insist they tag along. They compete for attention and sabotage each other. But these mutinous heathens have to live together.

"And when you're at your lowest, beaten, battered, and hopeless, you must march to the family dinner table and sit right next them and make nice – every night! That's where you learn to compartmentalize!" Cara screams.

She finally stands back, stepping away from Sasha, and takes a deep breath, "Don't you see, Sasha, you missed that class growing up. You never got the invite to that one. I am truly sorry about that. But you got the chance and attended the class, later. Pity, you didn't get a very good grade in it."

Sasha's face grows confused. Cara enlightens him. "Here, dipshit, for the last 15 years. WE are a family; you're like my brother. We tease, we beat on, we rip, and then we come to the table, and we LOVE! We love because that's what you learn in a family. You learn that despite what you've done, or what you intend to do, we LOVE YOU!"

Cara steps forward once again, and stares down at Sasha. "Get up, give me a hug, and tell me you love me, NOW!"

Sasha jumps up, but Cara doesn't give him a chance. She grabs him firmly and holds him for a few seconds before pushing off and getting back into his face. "YOU have 15 minutes to get your act together and I expect you at the dinner table, capisci stronzo?"

She must be really pissed when instead of saying the phonetic "capeesh," Americano style, she tells him, do you understand, asshole, in real Italian.

Sasha is at a loss for a moment. He hesitates before turning on his heel and heading to the stairs for the lower level.

Cara whips her head towards the two members of her audience. "Who's next?!"

Nic quickly scampers away, but as Reed watches Nic run out the garage door, he decides to make his way into the living room. Cara has her head down, shoulders slumped, looking utterly wiped.

He wraps her up in his arms and whispers in her ear. "Ya done good, sweetheart. Broody needed a kick in the pants. He was spiraling out of control."

Cara wraps her arms around his waist and leans into him as she exhales, letting all the rage drain from her system. At the same time, he lets go of all his warmth and love for her. Slowly, she melts into their embrace.

He takes her face with both hands, forcing her eyes to his. "You are still standing on your own two feet, even after everything that's happened today, and you have accomplished so much." Leaning in, he brushes his lips to the side of her mouth and whispers, "As usual, you couldn't make me prouder, my sweetheart."

He sweeps her off those two feet and carries her back to the family room to get comfortable on his lap in front of the fire. He needs to take care of her. Just like he has always done from the beginning.

CHAPTER 11

EVERYONE ASSEMBLES FOR DINNER, INCLUDING Sasha. Cara decides to stay by his side in case she needs to comfort him during the meal. The dinner conversation is kept away from the impending threats and focuses more on the children. The kids share what Carter has taught them about different video games he plays. They talk about schoolwork and upcoming games, recitals and concerts. Weirdly, they do most of the talking, an unusual role reversal, as if they recognize the discussion must remain light. Even Elijah offers some discourse.

After dinner, Jinx promises the teenagers dessert but in an hour. They clean up quickly, while Jake delivers pasta and bread to the agents outside. When he returns, they sit to watch the uploaded video. Jake has only found one with Sasha and none with Nic. The kids had only flubbed up once. Although, she and Nic are shocked to find out that both Max and Elijah had posted over 24 videos. Jake confirms they were all removed.

Jake sets the video to play on the flat screen in the family room. The six of them get comfortable and watch as Max appears doing his best Michael Buble, singing Sinatra's Fly Me to the Moon. Mia is on piano while Eli is playing the bass. In the background, Sasha is playing an acoustic guitar.

Cara keeps her eyes on the Sasha in the video, while her mind cues into the Sasha sitting next her. Video Sasha is playing but watching the kids; a smile and absolute pride showing on his face. The look of cherished love is so evident.

Sasha, I'm feeling your distress level. Please share.

You need to get out of my head, Vizzini.

Impressed he was able to clearly respond to her, mentally, Cara pushes, *Make me.*

Sasha leans in close to Cara and emits a low growl in her ear. *I'm not ready for more intrusion today, please.*

Deciding to extend him the mental privacy, Cara whispers, "Fine, then share with me or share with the group, because I know this is affecting you. How did she find this and why?"

When the video is complete, Sasha clears his throat and explains, "I used to play this song for Katherine on an acoustic guitar. It's the first song Nic taught me to sing and play. She loved it when I sang it to her." He looks wiped out just from that statement.

"That makes sense then," Jake states. "The video is over a year old. It's categorized on YouTube as an 'acoustic version'. Katherine probably just happened on it in search of the song. From there she could have investigated the names listed for the kids. They didn't place Sasha's on the video, but they did use their own when they set up their YouTube channel."

Reed takes over the conversation offering up what he has learned from his analysts at Langley. "Apparently, an inmate matching the description of the Camry man was charged with a B&E eight months ago in Connecticut. His name is Simon Joseff and he was incarcerated at the same prison as Ed Grotto. According to prison guards, Simon Joseff befriended Ed and remained in prison with him for almost 4 months. After that time, Joseff's attorney pulled the British citizenship card and got him released back to England." That happened a little over three months ago.

Reed also briefs them on his analysts' review of Customs and Immigration records since that time. Simon Joseff isn't listed as returning to the States according to their search, however, they're also looking for any possible cover names he may be using when he did come back. Reed's final piece of intel gets their undivided attention. "Simon Joseff spent seven years at the same institution as Katherine St. John in England. So, that's the connection."

"And Katherine?" Nic inquires.

Reed explains, "I am hitting some roadblocks on her. Because of whom her father is, I must tread lightly with my requests for information. Customs and Immigration don't report her in the States either, but it's likely she is here with a cover name similar to our suspicions about Simon. My analysts are searching through all phone records and possible addresses for Katherine in England, but it's a common name, and the process is slow," Reed declares. "I have reached out to the current MI6 Chief with a polite request but haven't heard anything yet. Her father Thomas' listed address and known records produced nothing of substance leading to Katherine."

Jinx admits she personally did a comprehensive search utilizing her login with the NSA. "I also came up empty," she admits.

"Does that mean he doesn't keep in contact with his daughter?" Cara questions.

"It would appear that way, based on his records," Jinx confirms.

Reed leans into Jinx and places a soft kiss on the top of her head. Jinx has been his finest analyst. His black hat. She could hack her way through any network. Such a critical component to his success, he thanked her by getting her the very high paying job she has now. Jinx has since repaid him by performing special favors over the years.

The NSA is not always quick or courteous in response to the CIA's request for access and, in fact, is sometimes a hindrance. A phone call to Jinx tended to remedy those situations. Just like now, without her, Reed couldn't even guess how long it would take to get approval for a search of those records. Because the NSA falls under the Department of Defense, the Director is a military General. The Pentagon is known for its secrecy, and its personnel play their cards close to their chest. They don't play nice in the sandbox with the other agencies.

Reed shrugs involuntarily, thinking about how much time he spends finessing the US military; more than he does running his own Agency. The Patriot Act gave the NSA carte blanche and they, in turn, left the CIA and the FBI in the dust. Concerned at any given time their funding might wane, the NSA maintains a stranglehold on its information and resources, purposefully choosing when to share these assets in a continuous effort to prove its worth. Reed often contemplates what this country could achieve if all the agencies remained apolitical, ended their turf wars, and actually worked together.

Reed's internal bitch fest is interrupted when Nic asks a question. Which, ironically, is the same type of bitching he does on a day-to-day basis with Nic's wife. Cara has been Reed's most valuable sounding board for ideas and resolutions. She even acts as his therapist.

Nic blurts out, "Setting aside the lack of any intel on Katherine's current whereabouts, we can establish her and Simon's activities fit into our timeline to have hired Vlad. But how do they connect Cara Andre, the married woman, to the intelligence agent known as the Reflex?"

Ed knew Cara as Cara Bianco. Katherine found Cara Andre through the kids' social media accounts. From there, making the connection between the two names was elementary. Things like marriage records, Facebook friends and phone records could be used for that. Once they connected the names, a search of 'Bianco' would have produced court records of her involvement in and connection to the Ed Grotto case. That information is public. But the Reflex? There's still no correlation whatsoever for that.

Also, if Katherine makes the Bianco/Andre connection, doesn't she already know where Cara lives? Maybe not an actual address, but she would know the general area to search. Why hire Vlad?

Reed looks to Cara for assistance but she appears exhausted. She doesn't make eye contact with him. Instead, she turns to push with her legs against the side of the slippery leather sofa, causing Sasha's body to give way enough for Cara to place her head down on his leg.

Sasha gives her a disgusted headshake before adding, "Katherine would definitely know where we live. As Cara Andre, she is listed as the owner of your design and construction business. The business is on enough websites and State and Federal lists to produce this address. I, too, utilize this address versus my apartment. By all appearances, we live together and share a last name. The underlying link we need to resolve is why Katherine would pursue The Reflex. Why hire Vlad to find the ex-agent? We need the reasoning behind that jump," Sasha adds with less emotion. He looks down with a reassuring smile at Cara's head on his lap. It's obvious to everyone in the room that Cara is staying close to him to feed him comfort.

"I really must be the weak link here. None of this makes sense. If Katherine can manage to trace your history all the way back to your involvement with Ed, doesn't she realize, Cara, you are married to Nic and not Sasha? Why hate you? You haven't betrayed her by taking Sasha from her," Jinx questions.

Nic proposes, "I don't think that's what's in her head. I think her hatred for Cara may come from producing the children Sasha loves so much. She's the vessel."

They all sit quietly for a spell processing all the information they've gathered and trying to come up with any new potential links.

Sasha has something to offer first. "Is Cara just a vessel, or is Katherine's hatred tied to the Reflex in some other way, or is it both?" He places his hand on Cara's forehead as he speaks. "Cara, did you ever work with any of the agents at MI6 during your tenure with the Agency?"

Cara looks to Reed to answer for her. The day has finally taken its toll on her. He responds, "Cara did work with many of the agents at MI6, and she spent considerable time there. Our agencies have always had very cooperative relations, more so then, than now, honestly. Why do you ask?"

With this acknowledgement, Sasha gently lifts Cara's head from his legs as he rises from the sofa. He places her head back down on the leather and stands to look at Reed and Nic. "Can we speak in private, Reed? You, me and Nic?" Interesting, Sasha did not invite Jake.

They follow Sasha out of the room without questioning. They pass Carter on his way into the kitchen.

Carter continues to the family room and sits in the spot Sasha vacated. He stares down at Cara sprawled on the couch. "Agent Bennett, your children have sent me to request their dessert."

Cara slowly lifts herself to a sitting position and studies him. "My children have sent you to do their evil bidding for them?"

Carter is about to come back with a derogatory retort of his own but stops himself. "You have wonderful kids, Agent Bennett. I'm very impressed with them. How you and Mean Man managed that is beyond me, but I compliment you."

Struck by his sincerity, she places her hand on his arm and thanks him. "And you know my name is not Chase Bennett, right?" Carter nods an affirmative. "Please, call me 'Cara' from now on."

Carter gives her one of his wry smiles. "Director Reed expects me to call you Agent Bennett."

"Carter, this is my house, my rules. While you're here, you will call me Cara. After that, you may decide what you're more comfortable with. Besides, you know I don't always adhere to Director Reed's rules." She gives him a wink. "You may still refer to my husband as Mean Man, though."

"Deal." Carter smiles, "Now, when are you serving dessert?"

Cara rises and heads to the kitchen to put out pie and ice cream for everyone.

CHAPTER 12

NIC ISN'T SURE WHERE TO lead them for some privacy. The kids are on the lower level, but he can hear Cara's thoughts so he knows they're looking to eat. He takes the chance and leads the other two men down to his office. As expected, Nic passes his two and Elijah on their way towards the stairwell after he descends.

"I hear there's pie and ice cream. Save us some." He reaches for Mia's hand, just brushing it, needing the contact after everything that's transpired.

Mia senses his need and doesn't pull away from him. Instead, she leans in and gives Nic a tiny peck on the cheek. God, he loves his kids.

Once in the office, Nic takes a seat at his desk while Reed sits in the plush chair. Sasha is pacing the length of the office before abruptly turning to Reed to ask, "How much do you know about the executed plan to keep Nic and me here in the States?"

Reed looks to Nic to acknowledge that some of those details were only just given to him on the plane ride the day before. "I heard of the initial plan where you killed Nic, and then you were killed by an agent from MI6sss." Reed lets the six-sound slur from his lips realizing why they are going to talk.

"Yes, precisely. Were you ever given the name of the agent who allegedly killed me?"

"At my level 15 years ago, I wasn't privy to that intel." Reed had heard the story and knew it wasn't true. Obviously, Nic was alive and well. Reed also knew how close Nic and Sasha had been. "Cara always made that clear. Looking back on it now, I realize she was preparing me for the truth of your presence here should it ever come out."

Reed shrugs his shoulders as he continues, "I always assumed you found a way out for yourself and rode off into the sunset." After some thought he adds, "I was curious as to who you found to cover for you at MI6, but to have investigated would not have been prudent. Don't forget, I was already harboring the crime of concealing Nic. I didn't need to call any attention to myself."

"I'm in a precarious position, Reed, and I need you to respect that," Sasha goes on, waiting for Reed to acknowledge.

When Reed nods subtly, Sasha confesses, "There was an agent in service for MI6, 15 years ago, who owed me a favor. This agent was... not always faithful to the Queen. He wasn't a double agent, per se, but he was reasonable. He and I developed a relationship over the years where we would sometimes share intel if one of our teams could be protected, or if the intel was dangerously inaccurate. We would squelch rumors. It was a mutual, working relationship, fully reciprocated. I had many of these types of associations."

Reed nods again in understanding as he maintains his own similar relationships, currently.

Sasha takes a deep breath before adding, "After what happened with Katherine, I came back a changed man. Rules, orders, and loyalties became more nebulous to me. I began to understand the need to separate the truth from the rhetoric. I developed my own rubric."

For some reason, Reed feels the need to interrupt Sasha. "You and I are very much alike. No one will understand the concept of judge, jury, and executioner more than me." He apologizes if he hasn't made it clear. "Sasha, I never believed you were the monster characterized by your reputation. Especially after I got to know Nic, who considers you a brother. I mean the man lets his wife be best friends with another man, and he hasn't killed me." Reed shudders slightly, "Early on I did think Nic might exterminate me." He shrugs and admits, "Instead, I respected and admired your expertise, skills and knowledge."

Nic did consider killing Reed. If he thought it wouldn't devastate Cara, the man would have perished. Over the years, he's realized how happy he is that he did not. Cara abuses Reed more than him. Connor Reed divides his wife's sass. Nic suspects Reed gets the brunt of it.

● ● ●

Reed laughs to himself for a moment, "And as for the creation of your own rubric? Well, in this country, it's called, 'Politics.' Welcome to my world. You don't need to explain or defend yourself, ever, with me."

Sasha studies Reed for a few moments. "Thank you…Now I should probably get to the point."

Reed assumes this is the reason they are sequestered in Nic's office without Jake. Sasha is going to reveal more counterintelligence secrets. It blows his mind to think of what has been shared in the last three days. Nothing short of treason.

With a deep breath, Sasha continues, "It's possible this contact who assisted me 15 years ago knew about the Reflex. Not because I came out and said it, but because the MI6 agent wouldn't strike a deal with me without some additional information. He wanted to know where I was going, why and with whom. He wanted the truth. When I told him I was working with Nic and what we were going to do, the Agent insisted on being the hero, protecting some poor civilian woman from the Dark Angel of Death. Apparently, he was concerned Nic's eternal love was going to damn this woman to Hell." Sasha makes a disgusted face at Nic. "I had to tell him the woman was a CIA operative. She could handle herself. He may have connected the dots."

Nic scowls at Sasha, "You never told me this."

Sasha glares back at Nic, "You did not need to know."

Reed smiles at the exchange. It's the first time he's seen Sasha act like the handler he was. "Sasha, if I'm connecting the dots correctly, you believe there's a possibility this man may have directly or inadvertently betrayed you by conveying this information to Katherine?"

"This agent is an old man, now. He's friends with Katherine's father, Thomas. He is also the man who was providing me with updates on her. Could Katherine have extrapolated this from information or stories he shared…yes. It's not much of a stretch. But why she needed to discover if Cara Andre was the Reflex is where I become confused. What's the motive? There is something more we're missing," Sasha admits.

Reed summarizes, "Katherine hears neither you, nor Nic are dead. You are in the US with Nic and the woman he married who happens to be former CIA. Best guess? She may have been told the agent is the Reflex. She may even have been given Chase Bennett as a name. Katherine then hires Vlad to confirm Cara and the Reflex are one and the same. At some point she received verification and released Vlad to kill her. Best case, Cara's dead. Worst case, her identity is confirmed one way or the other."

"Win/win, but why?" Nic looks to Reed. "Possible political ramifications?"

That's where Reed's leaning. It's one thing to go after one or two former KGB rogue agents. It's entirely another level of reprisal to hunt down and kill a former CIA agent and her children, potentially on her own soil. It must be the rationale behind the acquisition of Ed. Place him as the fall guy to placate any political backlash.

Nic shakes his head. "I like the reasoning, until Ed." He points to the flowchart and information up on one of his war boards. "Katherine could only have confirmed Cara as the Reflex on Friday, Thursday at the earliest. Ed was planned for and brought into the mix months ago."

"Back up plan for her if she received confirmation? I'm calculating a good probability for that," Sasha says.

Nic confides he's feeling strange. "Since the discovery of our gifts, the computations in my head have gone a bit off. The math is trying to fold in feelings. The equations that are trying to solve for variables are collecting sentiments through the threads, or through Cara's empathy. It's messing with my head. The probability of this scenario being entirely accurate right now, I'm calculating at less than 20%. Not because of finite math, but because of infinite variables added for the emotion."

Reed comes to Nic's aid, advising him not to fight it. His mind is weaving the emotion into the calculation as it should. It's the next progression for his grid. As they recently learned, all of Reed's intuition over the years has been based on his empathic ability. Nic shouldn't discount his advice. He just needs to give his mind time to adjust. "If you're calculating less than 20%, we are missing something."

"I have to concur," Sasha agrees. "Is it time for pie?"

Reed stands but turns to Sasha. "You weren't comfortable asking Jake to this meeting?"

They trust Jake for his loyalty to them and his skills. They don't trust Jake with information concerning their past, or their networks. "Without knowing whom Jake works for, or who he is associated with, we will not take that risk. Jake understands this. Without full disclosure on his part, there will always be some secrets between us," Sasha states.

"But you trust me with this?" Reed inquires raising one eyebrow at Sasha.

"We trust Cara. Cara trusts you. You get extension rights." Sasha cocks one eyebrow back at him.

Reed just stares at him for a moment longer before asking, "You're not going to tell me who your former MI6 contact is, are you?"

"No."

Reed adds, "You don't trust me enough with that intel, correct?"

"Yes."

At this admittance, Reed clasps Sasha by the shoulder and laughs, "Sasha, you would've disappointed me if you had trusted me!"

Before it all disappeared, Cara saved a slice of apple pie for Sasha and blueberry slices for Reed and Nic, their favorites. The guys added their ice cream and ate on the island stools. Cara waits until they're halfway done to let them know Jake and Jinx have gone home, explaining she assumes they wanted some alone time together. They left Eli to sleep over. The couple will be back bright and early at 8:30 AM.

"You haven't seen 8:30 AM on a Sunday since the kids were young, Cara. I can't believe you agreed to that," Nic teases.

Cara retorts, "I didn't. I said I would be sleeping. Jinx responded by telling me the world does not revolve around me. So, to spite her, I do intend to sleep."

"You look tired now, sweetheart," Reed comments concerned for her.

"I feel fried. Mentally. I asked Jake if that was, you know, normal for us."

Nic looks up at Cara. "What did he say? I feel the same way. Mentally spent."

"He said he's heard the gift can be overtaxed." Just then their landline starts ringing in the kitchen. "Nic, don't answer it, I can't talk to anyone right now." The phone rings four times, then goes to voicemail. The machine is on speaker; therefore, they can hear the message.

"Um, Cara, are you there? It's Danni. I've tried your cell, both call and text, and no answer from you. I had to resort to analog. Is everything okay there? Um, I'm somehow worried…"

Reed reaches for the phone and hits talk. "Danni, hey, it's Reed. How the hell are you?"

Because it's still in speaker mode, the group can hear the conversation.

"REED! OMG, it's been forever! Are you visiting Cara?"

"Yes, sorry, we've all been hanging out and having fun. Keeping your sister busy cooking and cleaning so she didn't see your calls or texts."

"Is everything okay there? I was suddenly…worried today and wanted to check in."

Reed looks to the group at the island who all register the same AHA moment on their faces. "Everything is fine. When do I get to see you again? Planning a trip to DC soon, I hope?"

"Nah, but maybe the next time I visit Cara, you can join us. I know Mr. Super Powerful is busy, but I always hope you remember us little peons who enjoy you for you."

This makes Reed smile. "Mr. Super Powerful? I like it, Danni. And 'peon' is not the word I would use to describe you."

"How would you describe me?" Danni asks playfully. Cara's sister is an in-demand marriage counselor in Connecticut. She is also an incessant flirt. She assumes Danni does not show her clients that side of her.

"Um, HOT. You still married to that unworthy of your great beauty and wit man?"

"Yes…but you are my first exception, Reed," Danni purrs.

"Exception?"

Cara is already shaking her head in disgust, making her way to the phone. Her sister, Danni, has even fewer filters than she does. Reed pushes away from her.

"Yeah, you know, exception. I get to pick two guys I can have sex with, and my husband gets to pick two women. We made our list when we got married. You're my first exception and let me tell you, I saw you while I was channel flipping on CSPAN the other day, and I'm still pleased with listing you as my exception from 10 years ago when I married."

"I'm flattered, Danni, and I believe I'll be taking you up on the offer. But out of curiosity, who is your second exception?"

"That would be Sasha. My sister knows how to pick'em. Lucky bitch."

At this revelation, Sasha is completely humiliated dropping his head down to hide his reddening face. Cara is practically climbing Reed to get to the phone. Danni has always flirted with both men over the years.

Nic decides to intervene, grabbing Cara and pulling her away from Reed, because the conversation is too entertaining to stop.

"So, who are your husband's exceptions?"

"He's a dimwit. He chose Jessica Alba and for some strange reason, Diane Sawyer. Like that's going to happen. I went with viable and available. So, you just let me know when. I figure someone in this family should take you out for a real ride, if you're up for it?"

Reed delivers his words slowly, and dripping with sexuality. "I promise you, Danni, it will be one hell of a drive."

"I'm counting on it. Has my sister heard enough yet? Is she completely mortified? I'm on speaker, am I not?"

Reed rolls his eyes and hands the phone to Cara, who grabs it, changes the setting to take her sister off speaker, and puts the receiver to her ear.

"You're an ass, Danni." Now they can only hear Cara's side of the conversation. "Yes, Sasha turned red, and yes, he still looks hot in that shade." She winks at Sasha. "And you are warned, Danni, you can't tell Reed shit like that. He won't hesitate to take you for that 'drive.' Although, I'm guessing it would be more fast and furious than long and pleasurable."

Reed flips her off and Nic giggles.

Cara tells her sister she's busy with a full house all weekend and she'll call on Monday. She hangs up and turns back to the group in the kitchen. "So, it seems it's very possible everyone in my family has some gift. They're too far away to make any connections from here, but Danni somehow knew. Reed, you'll eventually need to do some prying with your own sister. I wonder if there's something there, too?"

"You know Olivia and I have regressed to only a cordial relationship at best," Reed spills with some regret.

"I think your sister is very nice, despite her uber position in Manhattan high society."

Reed and his sister are very much alike but Olivia has managed to lose her sense of humor along the way. Cara blames Olivia's husband for that. Eugene is so uptight and boring. He's rubbed off on Olivia.

"My sister never had a sense of humor. That's the problem." Reed exhales as he states this. She knows that is not true. It's Reed's regret talking. He and his sister were close when Cara first met Olivia. She and Olivia are closer in age, and until Oliva met Eugene, they often went out together as a threesome. Olivia was fun, gorgeous and enjoyed making trouble. Then she met Eugene, who is not attractive but very wealthy and connected. Not that the Reed family require more wealth or affluence. Cara never understood the attraction. Olivia changed slowly after she met him. She became distant and superficial. Speaking of Oliva, Cara remembers the last text she sent begging her to plead with Connor about a blind date she wanted him to go on.

"Is she still trying, desperately, to get you to date that Isabelle woman?"

Nodding his head, a defeated Reed offers, "Yup, she still is."

Isabelle Harrison was seventeen years old the last time Reed saw her. Cara went with him to his cousin Peter's wedding, like 22 years ago. Isabelle sat on the other side of Reed at the dinner reception.

"Do you remember her?" Reed asks.

For some reason Cara has never forgotten her. She was a super skinny, no boobs, tall, redhead with hair in her face. "Poor girl, so shy and withdrawn. I don't recall if she even spoke during dinner. What ever happened to her?"

"Some sort of academic now, PhD in something boring. I don't want to ask and show any interest in her. If I opened that door, and Olivia had her way, she'd have me dating every pretentious, dull, rich woman in New York."

"Jeez, Connor, speaking of pretentious...some of those women may offer more than you give them credit for, sweetheart. I am standing up for all of them when I say give them a chance," Cara announces with pride.

"How utterly feminist and considerate of you. So out of character for Cara Callous," Reed ribs.

Cara juts her chin out at him. "Maybe I'm turning over a new leaf with today's epiphanies. I'm going to be kinder and more welcoming...ah, who am I kidding, that ain't happening."

"Truer words have never been spoken," Nic declares with great flair, reaching for his wife.

Cara jumps onto her husband's back. "Sasha, you and Reed have clean-up duty. Nic and I need to go have a much overdue conversation with our progeny."

CHAPTER 13

NIC AND HIS WIFE FIND the three kids with Carter in the Music room. Nic gives Carter a quick nod before asking if they can borrow Max and Mia for a few minutes. Carter, responding with a knowing glance, offers to keep Eli company and work some chords on the bass together. Eli only offers a faint smile. A smile is an affirmative from Elijah.

Nic motions his two out of the room, leading them around the corner into his office. When they enter, Nic places himself on the floor in the center of the room sitting with his legs out in front of him. Cara shuts the office door and joins him, sitting with her legs crossed. They wait for a moment before Max and Mia conclude they are supposed to get comfortable on the floor across from them.

Nic begins, but he no longer feels patient, he feels like a parent. "Why didn't you ever tell us, and did you know we had the same gifts?" Max and Mia start to look to each other, but Nic leans in as they do. "DO NOT SPEAK to each other! You will not discuss this between yourselves. If I even sense you're communicating, I will invade your minds, privacy be damned. I want the truth, not some agreed upon riposte from you both."

It's Max who speaks up first. He apologizes, but states he and Mia were always able to speak to each other. "Then, we found out Mia could speak to Eli. We didn't think it odd at first. It wasn't until we started school that it became more a freaky thing. Because we could never read you, Uncle Sasha, or Eli's parents, we thought all little kids could do it, but the adults had somehow outgrown it. We could sense some emotions from all of you, but we thought it might just be physical cues.

95

"You know, like when Mom is about to lose it, it shows on her face," Max uses as an example. "When we started school, that's when it hit us, we weren't like the other kids. And you weren't like the other adults. We began to hear everything and everyone."

Cara inhales sharply at this admission and Nic can sense her stress level increase, but she doesn't interrupt.

Mia starts in, "Mom, you're doing the face right now. STOP! On top of seeing it, now, since this morning, I can FEEL your distress."

Mia shudders at her mother before adding, "When we realized we could hear the chatter in everyone's mind, we all didn't handle it the same way. Max learned quickly to filter it. For some reason, his brain could, and still can, turn it off completely. I had more problems with it though, and that's when I decided to try and tell you about it." She points to her mother.

Cara's face falls at this news. Mia can see her mother searching her memories for the years ago moment she can't recall. "Mom, let me help."

Cara jolts as the memory is deposited into her mind. Nic lowers his head to watch it play through his wife.

It's their kitchen in their old house. Cara has just returned from taking the kids to see The Incredibles *at the movie theater. Mia is coloring and Max is on the floor with his Legos. Cara is busying herself making dinner. Mia calls out to her mother, "Mom, did you like the movie?"*

"Yes, honey, it was one of my favorites, so far. It was funny and I really liked the storyline. Did you?"

"Ahhh, I LOVED it. I wanna see it again." Little Mia pauses watching her mother cook. You can see her beautiful face preparing itself. "Mom? Is that real? You know, how people can have secret lives and superpowers?"

Much younger Cara stiffens immediately at the question, standing with her hands in the sink. The reaction is evident in her body language. She seems to compose herself before responding. When she turns to her daughter, her face is reflective and somewhat sad.

"My sweet girl, everyone has secrets, sometimes secret lives, and secret talents. Secrets are easy to hide...but superpowers? No."

The memory fades to a new scene. Cara is shaking her head comprehending the confusion Mia must have experienced at her long-ago reaction and response.

The scene starts with Nic pushing Mia on the swings at the park. He is laughing as Mia screams, "Higher, higher!"

Sasha is swinging Max in the air like an airplane while Max squeals, "I'm flying!"

Suddenly Mia yells to her father, totally out of context, as young children are prone to do. "Daddy, I loved the movie yesterday, can we see it again with you?"

Nic smiles warmly at his daughter, his hair longer and all golden blonde with some loose strands hanging in his eyes, blown there from the wind. "Yes, darling, we can see it whenever you like."

Mia yells to her uncle, "Sasha, will you come with us next time?"

While swinging Max, Sasha calls out to her, "As you wish, Buttercup."

Mia screams, "Yeeeaahhh! You're going to LOVE it, Sasha. It's about parents with secret lives!"

Younger Sasha almost drops Max, grabbing him just before he hits the ground. You can see him clutch Max to his chest, walking quickly towards Nic. Sasha's face has panic written all over it.

Mia registers her uncle's shock and says, "Daddy, I wanna stop now."

Nic grabs her on the pass back and brings her to a stop. She jumps off and looks at her father and uncle with her little serious face. "You will like it, Uncle Sasha, I promise. The mommy and daddy keep a big secret from their kids. They were superheroes before they got married and had them."

Nic's body stiffens as he pulls Mia tight to his leg while looking at Sasha, his eyes wide and frozen.

Mia squirms out of his grasp and gazes up at her father. "I know it's okay to have secrets. We can hide our secrets really good. But I know there are no superpowers. That part is just make-believe." Nic and Sasha continue to stare at one another but say nothing in response.

When the memory is over, Cara looks to her husband, whose face is guilt ridden. She isn't sure whether he's feeling her emotions or experiencing his own.

She takes a slow, deep breath and faces her children. "So, you thought based on our reactions, we knew, and preferred you not talk about it? Keep it a secret?"

Mia glares at her mother. "Yeah, like it was some special thing we had that we were never supposed to talk about. A secret just for us. Mom, I was 5 years old."

That's what they interpreted back then. Of course, after last night and the big secret agent reveal, the twins did finally figure out why their parents and Sasha had reacted the way they did. It had nothing to do with hiding their talents. Their parents didn't know about them. Mia continues, "We thought long and hard about it all night after your meltdown. We considered everything we could derive from the conversations around the house. Finally, we decided it was time to say something about our talents, but we never had to. Uncle Reed took care of that for us this morning," Mia concludes.

Nic responds, "But Mia, as you guys got older, didn't you question the 'secret' idea?"

Mia puts her head down at this inquiry. Suddenly, Cara feels it, the emotion, and the thoughts coming from her daughter. Just a small drip like Mia has formed a tiny crack in a dam.

Mia did think about it, often, but like Max, she enjoyed the consequence of her parents' cluelessness. School was easy for her. She didn't have to do any work. Mia learned to dim down the voices at school. She kept to herself. She adapted. She could hear the teachers talk about her. They wanted to recommend a better school for her, one offering even more challenging classes. Mia didn't want to leave Max and Eli.

"You thought we would send you away from us, split you up from your brother and Eli," Cara recites as these revelations enter her mind.

Cara takes a deep breath and tells her children they have nothing to feel ashamed of. She and their father, on the other hand, do. She admits when she was their age, she would have handled it exactly as they had done. And on some level, it's what she did. "But this is out now, in the open between us, and no more secrets, got it? We're going to proceed as if this is ground zero. Full disclosure from here on out."

Cara stops and looks to Nic before she adds, "Well, full disclosure with the nine of us, only." It still must be treated as a secret to the outside world. No one in the general public is prepared to accept their gifts. They may never be ready for that. It's their communal secret, now.

"As a rule, we will respect your privacy and not intrude on your thoughts, but in the event of need, all bets are off. We WILL intervene. I expect the same from you two. You give us our privacy but reach out to us at any time if you need us. Are we in agreement?" Nic urges.

As the children nod and start to stand, Cara stops them. The way they rectified this revelation about themselves is still bothering her. "I need to understand. What did you guys think was the reason you had these gifts?"

Max starts howling with laughter as Mia pushes him over. She's trying to cover her brother's mouth. All Max can get out is, "The Great Debate!"

Their father gently pulls Mia's hands from her brother's face. "Tell us." There is a compulsion to his request.

Sitting upright, while Mia crosses her arms, Max admits, "When we were really young, Mia decided we were witches." Cara's son looks to her. "Because you always called Nonna a witch."

Okay, that's true, but not necessarily meant literally about her mother.

Before Cara can contemplate more, Max continues, "Later, Mia began to read all kinds of Paranormal books. She then decided we were mages."

"Like sorcerers or wizards?" Nic asks.

Mia cuts her brother off. "Yes. And no, not like Harry Potter crap. More based on the Wicca faith. I started there with their pagan based beliefs and looked more deeply at the Druids, their history and practices. The elemental aspect of their rituals intrigued me." She shrugs, "Max was convinced we had the Force." Mia shudders at her brother. "The Force is elemental as well. It's essentially all the same. We are tied to our Earth and the forces around it."

Finally letting her brother speak, Max continues, "We always see or read something new and alter our conclusions. I do like to watch fantastical movies and science fiction because I think I can gain some clues. Mia does the reading."

Rolling her eyes, Mia adds, "I've been studying physics more now. Like Jake explained, it's all theoretical, but possible."

Knowing her husband has a dozen scientific questions, Cara jumps in before he can speak. What she needs to know is more important than the why. "Have the three of you played with, tested, or experimented with your gifts?"

Both of their heads drop before Mia cants hers offering, "We have been...reluctant...to do that." She picks her head up to face them both. "What I did this morning to you three was a test. I...am sorry. But the result is why we do not experiment."

With relief and understanding, Nic interjects, "You three needed a monitor or a control for any experiments."

Mia confirms, "Yes."

"I am pleased you are astute enough to understand the dangers of experimentation. Let us neutralize this current threat. If you feel you can assist, please let us know, otherwise, when we are done, let's plan on working as a family to investigate our gifts," Nic proposes.

Apparently, the discussion is over as both her children and Nic stand. Cara motions Mia to stay while Nic and Max walk out of his office together.

"Mia, one last thing. I can see your thread to Eli, and I see it isn't like the others between us. It is not a thread." Cara looks long and hard at her daughter before continuing, "The connection you have with Eli resembles the one I have with...your father."

Mia snaps at her, "I'm not ready to have this conversation with you, Mom."

"I know, and this conversation will only be between you and me. When you're ready to go there, please know you can talk to me. That's all I'm going to say on it."

Mia nods her acknowledgment and leaves her mother sitting on the floor in Nic's office.

Cara pulls her knees to her chest and places her head down on them. She is so drained. So much is flying around in her mind. The three days of threats, confessions, reveals and discoveries are playing with every nerve in her body.

Looking at her wristwatch, she realizes the last 16 hours were the longest and the shortest of her life. From a jog on the course, to finding out gifts exist, to using said gifts, to finally finding out why Sasha is emotionally stunted, to discovering who is after them and why, and concluding with bad mommy guilt. Existential, surreal, amazing, and disappointing. She sighs and rubs her temples.

Her consciousness literally looks like it's spinning. Now that she can draw herself into it, the visual in her mind is startling. There's a section of her consciousness moving in a funnel cloud. Cara snorts to herself. She has always said her mind is swirling, never realizing her brain quite literally does.

She's so inside her mind watching the vortex, she doesn't notice the legs standing before her. Cara looks up to see the painted footprints of Sasha's Just Dance pants, evidence of Mia's handiwork in decorating his clothes. The images grow closer before his hands pull her gently towards the chair behind her.

Sasha gets down on the ground and pulls Cara under his arm and leans them back against the chair together. He just leaves her to her thoughts.

When he feels she's ready, he says, "You did well with the kids. Despite what you may think sometimes, you're a great mom, Cara. You and Nic are doing a tremendous job so far. I know the next phase appears more daunting, but we, as a family, will get through it."

Cara looks up into Sasha's eyes. "I am sorry for the tough love earlier. It felt like the natural direction to take."

"It was. And you have no need to apologize. I need some time to sort it all out. I've lived with this anguish and guilt for a very long while." Sasha glances up to see they're facing the war board with the flowchart. He stares at it in silence before asking, "Do Katherine and I have a thread?"

"Everyone is threaded but, no, you two are not connected by a thread like all of us are with you." Cara pauses, not sure how she should proceed. "Katherine wasn't supposed to be in your life. I feel her presence again, and it isn't scripted, if such a thing exists."

"You think the six of us were always meant to find each other?"

"Yes. What drew you to Nic? Do you recall?"

Concentrating, Sasha finally says, "I heard about the new boy. Some of the instructors said he was extremely intelligent. But the gossip amongst the boys was Nicolae was a useless, weak, pretty face. I don't understand why I went looking for Nic, but I felt compelled to find him and meet him. When I did find him, I knew I had to help him." He looks down at her. "Is that what it's like, compulsion?"

"In various degrees, yes. I see it that way."

"Did you feel that with Reed?"

"The moment I met him, I knew he was meant to be a part of my life."

"You know I still don't fully comprehend your relationship with Reed."

A second involuntary snort comes from Cara. Her relationship with Reed isn't what she feels like talking about. It's never what she wants to discuss because it's not simply a conversation. For 25 years, Reed has been a demanded explanation. There was Nic constantly badgering her, her family incessantly teasing that Reed must be gay, or their superiors at work insisting they come clean about their couple status. Cara has spent the better part of her life mounting a defense when it comes to Connor.

Their relationship is odd. Neither would ever deny that. How it got that way and why can be debated. In the end, though, Connor was Cara's whole world before she met Nic. And after, he was no longer her world, but she could never live without him in it. Reed fills a void and a need even Nic and the kids can't. Maybe it's because they have so much history together? Cara has never been sure why, but his importance to her life she will not question.

She focuses back in her mind at all of the threads. Reed's thread to her is so interesting. After examining it, Cara turns her attention back to Sasha. "Can I be honest with you?" Sasha nods slowly. "Unlike our thread to the others, the diameter of the thread between you and Nic resembles the thread between Reed and me. There are other differences, but the thickness is the same. I'm not going to ask you to talk about your feelings, but it makes me wonder…if Nic had been a woman, what would you have expected of your relationship?"

Sasha contemplates this interesting concept for a moment before turning seriously to Cara. "Nic would be my bitch. I would've kept him tied to a bed for my sexual pleasure most of the day." She plugs him in the chest. "Okay, maybe that's extreme."

Laughing, Sasha admits, "I had beautiful agents reporting to me. I was their handler, and I was very protective of them. I never slept with them, but I don't believe I was threaded to any of them. Although there was one once, right before I came here to see Nic when I heard about your pregnancy…" He doesn't finish his sentence and goes back into thought. When he opens his mouth next, nothing comes out.

His mouth closes and reopens with, "If Nic had been a woman, maybe it would be like you and Reed. That's what you're trying to make me understand?"

"Yes, but I wanted your honest answer, you know, for posterity." Cara smiles, referring to yet another quote for him from *The Princess Bride*. "I think the fact Reed and I aren't the same sex makes it more complicated. His emotional connection, coupled with the testosterone, causes his feelings for me to become indistinct. And…," poking Sasha as she completes her thought, "at least my handler doesn't live with us."

Sasha considers his words before speaking. It's been bothering him since last night. After today's epiphanies, it's disturbing him more. He's already spoken to Nic about it, not because he was trying to cause trouble, but because he was very concerned that Nic also believes what Sasha suspects about Reed. The man adores her. Reed reveres her. Sasha can see beyond their biting repartee with each other. There is a deep devotion there. "You are aware Reed's in love with you."

Cara doesn't jump at him as he expected. She simply sits with her head on his shoulder for a pause before her head drops in defeat. "He THINKS he's in love with me."

"Is there a difference?"

"Very much." She inhales, as if for patience. "If Reed were truly in love with me, we would have been a couple."

Deciding that's a loaded statement, Sasha goes quiet. But Cara changes direction. "Like you with Katherine in a way."

"I don't understand."

"She was your first girlfriend, really. The first time your emotions and body experienced the thrill of passion. It doesn't mean it is love; it really is more physical desire. It can be confusing to someone with little experience."

"Are you saying Reed is inexperienced?" Sasha asks with a little mocking in his voice.

Cara looks at him disapprovingly, before attempting to elaborate for him. "I am quite sure Reed has a lot of sexual experience, but that's all he's had. His relationship with me is opposite of what you had with Katherine. I have been Reed's single source of emotional connection. He's never had another emotional relationship with a woman. That can be confusing. There's all this love pouring between us, yet the physical portion isn't there.

"Honestly, had I not found Nic, it may still be confusing for me to understand. With Nic, the emotional connection was definitely there, but the physical connection…that was intense. No questions, no conjecture, no hesitation. I can see and feel the difference, now. Reed just hasn't found both yet to be able to understand the distinction."

Thinking about this confession, Sasha recognizes the truth in it. He sees the similarity to his relationship with Katherine. He found the physical with Katherine, but the emotional connection never existed. It was only the hormonal lust of the young and inexperienced. Quite typical and appropriate, according to Cara. The real issue for him now is guilt over the tragic outcome. It's prevented him from forming any emotional ties to another woman. He doesn't need Cara to say that aloud. He can sense all her thoughts in his mind, loud and clear.

"You don't believe I have an emotional connection to you?" Sasha asks her, concerned.

"Yes, of course we have that connection, but our relationship is different. You and I, Sasha, we are family."

He does feel like a brother to her, but even better than that. He comes with all the benefits of having a brother but without the sibling torment she experiences in her constant squabbles with her real brother, Robert. He wonders…if they had met before she encountered Nic, would their relationship be as confusing as hers and Reed's?

Cara smirks at his musings because she is listening inside his mind, uninvited. "For some reason I think we would've been close but not sexual, either."

"I would have tied you to a bed as well, and made you my sex slave," Sasha quips but pauses for a moment to admit, "I feel more protective and loving with you, the way I assume a brother would of a younger sister." He gives Cara one of his rare ear-to-ear grins. "I have a confession to make. When I came to meet you for the first time, I was convinced I wouldn't like you. I had heard the stories of the famed Duo, and you didn't seem like the kind of girl I would've wished for Nicolae. It didn't take long to see I was so wrong, however. Not because of the love you have for each other, but for who you really are. You are not what you like to project. You are capable of great compassion and loyalty. You altered the course of my life and made it worth living. You're still doing that."

Cara tries not to react to Sasha's confession. She doesn't want him to feel uncomfortable about sharing his emotions. She knows she needs to stay silent as positive reinforcement for what she understands is a difficult task for him. She sits still with her head against his chest and his arm around her shoulders.

"Sasha, thank you for sharing and...well, you're giving me energy while we sit here. I'm feeling much better. Did you know you were doing that?"

"Yes...I'm beginning to recognize the ability." Sasha states with earnest. "Cara, can I ask one more question?"

"Shoot."

"Funny pun. I'm sensing the guilt you're feeling about your connection to Reed. Are you thinking you need to assuage that guilt somehow?"

Cara doesn't hesitate. Reed means so much to her, but up until today, it was easy to be in the Land of Denial about his emotions, and her monopoly of them. Reed deserves so much more. And like Sasha, she's concerned he has missed an opportunity to connect to the correct thread. She believes IF they meet the one, they will know. But she considers she can't trust that to happen. Cara is still not sure that's even possible for them. Her only experience to draw on is Nic.

"In my head, the empathy and telepathy still fight with the plain old thinking portion of my brain. That part of my brain is racked with guilt. And I'm carrying enough guilt because of all of this." Cara waves her arms to encompass the war board and the whole house.

"I'm beginning to think I can feel enough to understand. You know if you need me for anything, just ask." He draws her closer with this statement.

She suddenly feels compelled to share a thought. "What your organization did to you all those years ago with Katherine was a horrible thing. Had your cover never been blown, you could be married, a father, and potentially working at MI6 as a double agent. Your whole life was mapped out for you without your consent. You could have been stuck in a loveless marriage where you resented your wife and potentially your kids."

Placing her hands on each side of his face, she continues, "Sasha, the best thing that could have happened was what occurred. Yes, Katherine was injured but you were saved. It may not feel like that but it is the truth."

Sasha sighs out slowly, "I do understand that, Cara, but you of all people know the demands that are placed on us working in counterintelligence. In Russia, it's a lifelong commitment one way or another, and one does not deny a direct order."

Before she can retort, he adds, "And don't try to tell me the CIA hasn't been as ruthless in its methods over the years."

She is left only blinking at him. He is correct, of course. Cara is ashamed she was part of the organization at times. The CIA was so politically motivated during the last decades. The decisions they made and the things they did were nothing short of criminal. Look how many Central and South American countries have been manipulated by the CIA, and what happened in the Middle East that eventually brought down the Twin Towers. She could go on and on and all of it makes her sick.

She and Reed were never a part of that, however. Their team was allowed to fly solo as long as they achieved results. And those results... they determined... only them. If massaging the truth was what was required, that's what they did. Even after she left, Reed kept up the ruse. He manipulated the organization so their efforts were viewed as worthwhile and successful - because they actually were. That effort, and the hard work that came along with it, just may not have been exactly in line with the agenda outlined for the mission or the organization.

Sasha whispers into her ear, "I hear those thoughts. You understand I did what I could within my group, too."

Snapping at him, she says sharply, "Because you were there! You didn't die in London undercover. You did the right thing and saved yourself. Then you went back to Moscow and made a difference!" Grabbing a fistful of his shirt, she expounds, "You rewrote the script. You probably saved countless altercations from occurring. You might have saved the world for all we know. Can you not appreciate what you did achieve?"

Huffing out, Sasha states, "You make me sound like a hero."

Shaking him, Cara tries again, "You *are* a hero. I see both you and Reed that way." She gives him a big hug. "Just think about that as well, when you reconcile all of this, okay?"

Now he is left only blinking and speechless. Deciding he needs to mull over this new nugget for a minute, she moves back into her original position under his arm. She can hear and feel his muddled thoughts and emotions. When his brain seems to quiet, she releases her final concern.

"Sasha, one more thing," Cara sits up and turns her body towards him, so they're face to face. "I will kill Katherine. Are you emotionally prepared for that?"

Sasha takes a large breath before speaking, "Cara, I'm prepared to destroy her."

CHAPTER 14

CARA WANDERS THE LOWER LEVEL. Sasha has gone to his room wanting some private time. Carter is out of the music room and watching a movie with Far Guard and Max. There's a lot of exploding noises and guns but that's all Cara can get from it because they need the special 3-D glasses they're wearing to view the screen. She takes the steps up and wanders the first floor. No one is around.

She goes up to the next floor and finds Mia and Eli in her room. They're at her computer watching Internet videos and laughing. Cara wants to walk in on them but changes her mind and walks towards the closed guest room door. She raises her hand to knock but decides against that as well. She moves back to Mia's door and knocks gently while calling out, "Don't stay up too late, promise?"

Her own bedroom is calling. She stops by the kitchen to grab bottled water and heads to bed. The door to the suite is closed. Cara quietly opens it to find Nic sitting on the floor in front of the lit fireplace in only his boxers. He appears zoned out. No lights are on in the bedroom, only the shadows of the flames flickering on the walls and his face.

She walks past him to the bathroom. She brushes her teeth, washes her face, and takes her clothes off. She makes her way back into the bedroom and sits directly behind Nic, spreading her legs until she has full contact with his back. She wraps her arms around his waist and leans her head on him.

They sit unmoving and quiet until Cara feels the memory she shared with Nic that morning come into her mind.

She must have fallen asleep after their first night together. She slowly awakens to the memories of the most amazing night of her life. The previous evening was the object of dreams, more passionate and sensual than she could have ever imagined. But suddenly, she feels confined. She is bound. No, no, it can't be true. He would want to hurt me after all? *Her heart is utterly breaking.*

As her eyes open, she realizes she is not bound, but wrapped in Nic's arms and legs so tightly, any movement is restricted. His head is in the crook of her neck and he's sound asleep. He is the most beautiful creature she has ever seen. Ethereal. His face and body are perfect, but her feelings at his nearness are intensely passionate. He had truly fallen from the heavens.

After a few minutes of admiring him, she cautiously tries to wiggle out from his grasp to go to the bathroom without waking him.

Just as she's free, he mumbles in his sleep. "Cara mia, don't leave me, please. Ever."

At that moment, looking at his face, she knows she never will.

Nic has wrapped Cara with his arms behind him as the memory played. He lets his hands run up the sides of her torso until he can't reach any further, drawing her tight to his back. Releasing his grip on her, he runs his fingertips down her arms slowly until they meet her hands at his waist. He wraps his hands around hers, tightly, and lets his memory flow to her.

It's the same morning and Nic has just completed a dozen rounds of lovemaking with her. He lifts his body from her to see she's sound asleep, completely exhausted. It's then he notices he has left some bruises and marks on her. He frowns and becomes upset. He gently kisses each bruise and red welt. He doesn't seem to notice the scratches and marks on his own body.

When he's done kissing each injury, he runs his hands over her face, softly, and moves her hair away. He places tiny tender kisses all over her face leaving her lips for last, lightly brushing his across hers. He slowly pulls her to his side, wrapping his legs and arms around her, needing her close. His last thought before falling asleep, Cara mia, don't leave me, please. Ever.

Still holding her hands, Nic brings them slowly up his chest and neck until they reach his face. He kisses each fingertip. Rising, Cara moves in front of him to straddle his lap. She sits comfortably and just stares into his eyes which are reflecting the flames behind her and burning crimson.

She gradually sees his grid as she enters his mind. He has dimmed the lights on it, so it appears like thousands of twinkling stars in the night sky. Instead of the dizzying sensation of his grid before, this version is peaceful. There is the serenity and veneration of gazing at the heavens. It's spectacular.

Caught up in the sight above her, Cara starts to sense his emotion, the intense love he has for her. She releases her own emotion to soar into his mind. The result is so overwhelming; they both inhale sharply. It's all there. All the love, trapped under the blinking, sparkling night sky of his mind.

Nic leans in with their special lip caress, but instead of deepening the kiss, he slowly lifts her and rises to bring them to the bed. He lays her down gently, caringly, bringing his body over hers. They take that long and pleasurable drive; but this drive is filled with the sights and sensations of seventeen years of wonder, respect, desire, and adoration.

With his arms and legs wrapped around her once again, just like on their first night together, Nic closes his eyes. The lovemaking was altogether divine, and his body is completely sated. Peace and sleep are awaiting him.

Suddenly, Cara jerks out of his grasp. His eyes do not need to be open to know she is sitting next to him with her knees up to her chest in contemplation. He is not going to be able to sleep. Finally, he acquiesces, "Baby, what's the matter?"

He pops one eye open to see her facing him. She is naked, but her position prevents him from seeing anything. Doesn't matter, she is still beautiful, maybe more so, with the freshly fucked glow to her. Despite the contented luminosity, her face is serious.

"Nic, I may not have been entirely forthright in my story of how I came to work for Reed."

Deciding he needs to be more upright for this, he props the pillows behind him. "You two said Reed invited you to lunch when you visited him, Jinx picked you up from Security, and then you were hired. New job, new roommate and a new name is what you said."

Canting her head at him, she states, "That part is all true, but...Reed never had any intention of hiring me."

"Okay. Did you omit something?"

Cara winces, "Kinda a big something." He just wanted to sleep. But now, the adrenalin has entered his system.

Placing his hand on her knee, he questions, "And you are going to tell me this big something, now?"

She nods, unapologetically. "I said on the plane ride back from Berlin, I was coming to DC to interview for a job at World Bank. That is true. It's what happened at that interview I didn't disclose."

Eyeing her carefully, Nic summarizes, "You hadn't seen Reed in a few weeks, you get this interview, and you go down and stay with him to attend. It's this interview that changes his mind?"

Sighing, she admits, "I am going to pull the memory of the interview and the evening after it. Will you watch it, please?"

There is tension coming off her in waves. He thinks back to when she and Reed were sharing their tale on the plane. She did prevent Reed from telling this story. Nic recalls her placing two fingers in her mouth. A signal? A sign between the two of them to skip the tale. Why? And it was his wife making the decision. Resigned, he requests, "Send me the memory."

Cara is in an office. She's being interviewed by a woman who is sitting across from her behind a desk. The woman is from Human Resources and she is explaining some general attributes of the World Bank job Cara is applying for. Cara is excited and elated over the possibilities of the position. Nothing she has interviewed for since she graduated college has been nearly this interesting. The pay is decent, and Cara believes she may really enjoy this job. The woman explains there will be extensive travel, much of it international, and asks Cara how many languages she can speak.

The woman appears impressed with Cara and tells her she would like the hiring manager to meet with her. They continue to talk before a man in his late twenties strolls into the office without knocking, casts a cursory glance at Cara and interrupts the interview.

He then turns to introduce himself to Cara, and while they are still shaking hands, he pulls her from the chair. He insists they have lunch and starts negotiating Cara away from the office, down the hall and out of the building to a café across the street. His hand on her arm, he never gives her a chance to protest.

They order their lunch, and he continues the interview, asking her questions about her background, experience, favorite subjects, favorite things to do when she isn't working. Once the food arrives, he begins to describe the position, but he keeps his explanation rather obscure.

Pretty soon, he's asking more personal questions. He explains the job would require a tremendous amount of travel, so he wants to know if she has a boyfriend or any serious relationships preventing her from keeping an open schedule. Cara tells the man she isn't in any kind of relationship, and nothing would inhibit her time. He nods approvingly, and then explains how important it is that his assistant and he get along very well because they would be spending a significant amount of time together.

Nic knows where this is going. He stares dead on at his wife. She simply nods for him to continue.

Cara asks the hiring manager how he intends to determine their compatibility. The man gets up, comes around to Cara's side of the table, pulls her from the chair, bringing her body against his. He leans into her and with a whisper proposes they meet at his place for dinner that evening to find out.

Cara sets a time for dinner with the letch, and leaves the restaurant, smiling.

"Please tell me you didn't." Nic breathes out.

"Just keeping watching."

The memory jumps to Cara walking into Reed's apartment. She immediately picks up the phone in his kitchen and calls him at work. With eerie composure, she relays everything that happened at the interview. She calms Reed down by the end of the conversation before asking him, "Reed, feel like helping me teach a bad boy a lesson?"

The memory jumps again... Cara is dressed to kill in fuck-me shoes, a skintight dress that leaves nothing to the imagination, and sultry hair and makeup. She looks incredible. She's walking down an apartment building hallway, heading to a door. She knocks and the hiring manager opens the door. The look on his face when he sees her is priceless. He is practically panting with desire.

He is speechless as he lets her into the apartment, so she starts talking first. "Do we plan to have dinner, or do you want to start with dessert?" She drops her eyes to take in the raging hard on, albeit the size of a stack of dimes, pushing out his trousers. She leans in and brushes her fingertips over his little bulge, just very lightly, and tells him, "I think dessert, first."

He still can't speak, so she adds, "You need to let me get my dessert ready." She starts to undress him, slowly unbuttoning his shirt and taking it off. She unbuckles his belt and pants, letting them drop to the floor. He steps out of them and remains where he is, wearing only his underwear. He leans in to touch her for the first time, but she backs away and tells him, "Please remove your underwear, because I need to admire the full view before you can touch me." He complies and is standing there completely naked when there's a knock on the door.

Cara heads to the door, before he can stop her, and opens it. Reed is there in just jeans with flip-flops on, no shirt and muscles everywhere. A young Reed with messy hair, body cut, and carved, and menacing. He walks in and shuts and locks the door behind him.

Poor little naked man is horrified. Cara offers, "This is my fuck buddy, Troy." He doesn't appear to understand her. She endeavors to clarify for naked hiring manager. "I can only fuck two guys at the same time because one guy is too boring for me. I can't get hot anymore with just one." Hiring manager looks panicked, so she says reassuringly, "It's going to be the best experience of your life."

Naked man is only slightly mollified until Reed whines, "I don't know, Cara. This one isn't of your usual caliber. He's so small. I don't know if he's going to do it for me."

"I know, but I'm making an exception in this case. I really want this job, and he may be fun. We won't know until we try."

"Fine, but he needs to suck my dick real hard, and then I can put it in his ass while you have your fun with him. Does that work for you?"

"I love to watch you get your cock stroked and sucked. You know it always makes me so hot and wet," she purrs seductively.

The hiring manager finally speaks. He begins to stutter, "I don't think I can do this," over and over. Meanwhile, Reed has unbuttoned his jeans and is pulling down the zipper.

Cara moves in real close to naked hiring manager and whispers in his ear, "Yes, you can, you're going to love it. I promise." Then she kicks his legs from behind, dropping him onto to his knees with his face inches from Reed's crotch. Reed grabs hold of the guy's head, holding his face directly in front of his pants. The moment the guy begins to struggle, Reed reaches out with lightning speed and cuffs his hands behind his back in a wire tie. He's so fast, you can't even see where he pulled the tie from.

Reed tells him, calmly, "Dude, don't fight it, you know you want to suck it. It's beautiful." Then he pulls down his jeans just enough to give him the full view. Hiring manager is close to tears. Reed studies him for a moment before he turns to Cara and states, "I think he's too upset for the blowjob. I should just put this in his ass and let's get this party started."

Grabbing the man's head and pushing him down, Reed has him on his knees with his ass in the air and his head on the floor. He spins around and gets into position to sodomize the asshole. By this time, the man is crying hysterically.

Cara discreetly places her purse next to Reed before she walks in front of the guy and gets down on her knees so she can be as eye level with him as possible. She picks his head up and tells him, "I need to see your beautiful face when Troy pleasures you, darling. How am I going to get wet if I don't?" And then on cue, Reed takes the biggest cucumber Cara could find at the small local grocery store from her purse, and places it against the guy's ass.

Naked hiring manager starts screaming. Cara frowns at him like it's just occurred to her he isn't having any fun. She asks, "You're not enjoying this? I'm so sorry but it's the only way I can get off." She pauses for effect before saying, "I guess this means I don't get the job?" He's frantic by this point. Cara gets up. Reed puts the cucumber away, zips up his pants, grabs her handbag and they walk out of the apartment leaving hiring manager cuffed, crying and convulsing.

Nic is shaking, with rage, with indignation, with horror and with exasperation. The only words coming from his mouth or mind are, "You planned the whole charade."

His wife shrugs before trying to defend herself. Nic stops her with his hand in her face. Her defense is not what he needs. He requires a moment to solve the enigma that is his wife.

Making her employment with the bank contingent on sex is nothing short of despicable. It's harassment at the highest degree and inexcusable. Having only survived a rape attempt months before, he could understand Cara's rage. She was only 20 years old when all of this occurred.

He is starting to comprehend the perplexity of the human jigsaw puzzle he married... a young woman, a civilian, able to channel her rage into such a diabolical plot to 'teach a bad boy a lesson', to humiliate the man, debase him so thoroughly, he most likely never harassed another woman again. It's no wonder Reed would want to hire her after that farce.

Part of the mystery of Cara is solved. It all started with her. The Duo was born that night. They could have extrapolated anything they wanted from that poor shlep. Anything. It's sick and brilliant all at the same time. Not sex as a weapon, but sex as a tool in an arsenal of manipulation and subterfuge. Forget Whore School. Sex as a seduction tactic has nothing on sex used to defile. And her plan, it prevented any blow back on them. Hiring manager was not going to admit he asked her over for sex. She and Reed held all the cards.

Nic looks at his wife with new eyes. By 20 years old, she must have become so accustomed to harassment, the emotional response became rote to her. She was and is a gorgeous woman. How many times was she placed in a position to defend herself?

And Reed, he capitalized on her abilities. Cara was a weapon 25 years ago he wasn't going to lose. He asked her to Langley for lunch the very next day and laid out his proposal. Cara had conditions, though. Now, knowing the full story, the outcome of those conditions makes sense.

Before he can continue solving his puzzle for more unknowns, Cara interrupts, "I can hear all your thoughts, Nic. And yes, Agent Connor Reed, not fuck buddy, Troy, visited naked hiring manager after my lunch at Langley. He blackmailed him into hiring me and giving me a paycheck, a desk, and a phone at World Bank. Naked Hiring Manager, whose name is Steve, received a new assistant who was never there."

"And a convenient cover is born," is all Nic can say.

Lowering her head, she admits, "Yes." Again, before he can say more, she adds, "I am sorry. I was not ready to divulge this information to you on the plane. Not only is it a breach of security, a breach of trust, and a breach of honor, I realize it's a hard pill for a husband to swallow."

Hard Pill? The idea his wife spent a decade with her boyfriend utilizing practices in their repertoire that included lots of physical contact? It's more than a hard pill. It's a revelation. No wonder these two have no physical boundaries with each other.

"We do have boundaries. No mouths below the waist and no penetration," Cara responds matter-of-factly to his thoughts. Then she adds, "And no one was ever allowed to touch me during a mission. Connor forbade it. I am for his hands only."

Of course, 'not even a scratch on you' Agent Connor Reed would never allow Cara to feel uncomfortable. He protected her. He had the skills, the power and the resources to do it.

As Cara finally drops her knees and lays next to him, she wraps her arms around his waist. Speaking into his chest, she states, "Reed always protected me. He still does. And you needed to understand that part of our relationship. More importantly, you needed to understand me."

She takes a deep breath before adding, "I will never allow sexual abuse or harassment perpetrated on myself or anyone I love. I lost my patience and tolerance for it a long time ago. I WILL get even. No hesitation. I wish more women in similar situations had my fortitude in confronting it head on, but I acknowledge not all have the means."

Scooching down so they are face to face, Nic wraps her up in his arms. Cara was almost gang raped in Kabul. He saved her. Or was it true that he had to come to her rescue because his grid jammed her sonar as Reed accused? But, then again, she was never supposed to be in Kabul. Reed did not know of, or approve of her mission. Strange. Or maybe just a weird irony they should meet then, there and under those circumstances.

Cara grabs his chin. "Don't. Don't think about Kabul. Maybe if you weren't there, I would have sensed them coming for me and killed them based on intuition alone. Maybe not. Doesn't matter. I found you. That's all that matters." She snuggles into him. Eventually, her breathing evens out.

Cara awakens to the sound of dogs barking, incessantly. Nic has her cradled against his chest. His legs and arms still wrapped tightly around her.

Nic? Can I have your gun to shoot the dogs?

Forget the dogs; I'm going over to shoot the neighbors. It's not the dogs' fault.

"How can they always do that? They leave them out there barking to wake the entire neighborhood. We should definitely at least kick their asses," Cara whines.

Nic presses his arousal against her bottom and between her thighs. He's been awake for a while watching her sleep and admiring, his thoughts a conflicting clutter of emotions. The journey with her in his mind last night was enlightening. He has always loved her with every molecule of his being, but to literally see and feel her complete and committed love for him was affirming. On the other hand, there are components in their love for each other that do not measure up to what his wife shares with her boyfriend. Obviously.

After she fell asleep, he let his mind wander through so many scenarios involving the two of them. The memories and revelations weighed heavily on him all night.

Cara and Reed share a love filled with respect, pride, and absolute faith in one another. Although Nic wants her to feel that same intense devotion for him, he is realizing this morning, he does not feel it for her, either. He respects Cara, and she makes him proud, but he doesn't have the kind of blind faith in her as he does in Sasha. That kind of reverence can only be earned. As successful mission partners, it's understandable that absolute trust would be a byproduct.

Cara asks, snapping him out of his deep, blocked thoughts, "What time is it?"

"7:30"

She sighs in disgust before leaning against him until he's on his back. She crawls onto his chest to sensuously rub her body across his. "Argh, so early...but you do feel good. How about I make you a deal? Let's finish this in the shower where I can't hear the dogs?"

"Sex before coffee? I'm making good progress with you. These new gifts are going to be very advantageous. You have yourself a deal."

By the time Cara is dressed for the day, Nic has already made coffee and is working on pancakes for the crew. He knows she's headed to the kitchen and has a large mug waiting for her. Nic hands it to her as she passes him, leaving a small kiss on his cheek. Although Nic's thoughts were blocked this morning, his emotions were not. She was afraid he would think her a deviant, but instead, she feels only resignation from him. The truth of her employment needed to come out of the closet of her mind.

With Ed Grotto running around out there, Nic needed to understand her compulsion for revenge against sexual abusers. She will find him and kill him, once and for all.

Seated at the table this morning are Jinx, Jake and Reed, all of them eating their pancakes.

Cara sits and watches as they wait for her to take some sips of her coffee before they give her any direct eye contact.

Once it appears safe, Jinx inquires, "The dogs again?"

"Yes, or I would still be asleep."

"When this is over, we need a plan of attack on those neighbors of yours," Jinx adds.

"Agreed. Are Carter and Far Guard sleeping in?" Cara inquires.

"It appears that way," Reed says admonishingly.

"I'm certain they were up late watching action movies downstairs with my son. Max can be a bad influence. Don't be too hard on them," Cara tries to soothe.

"Like mother, like son?" Reed looks right at her for the first time this morning.

Cara meets his eyes and smiles. She observes Reed has more casual clothes on, but soon notices they are beyond casual.

"Wait a minute, are you wearing an A & F T-shirt?" Cara implores with concern.

Reed rises slowly to reveal his fitted shirt and the jeans he's wearing. The jeans have colorful painted medieval shields, swords, and Templar symbols on them. Cara inhales when she recognizes them.

Reed smiles wide at her reaction. "I asked Sasha if I could borrow some clothes. I ran out. Apparently, he has a very keen sense of irony."

"Apparently. Another favorite show, the BBC's *Merlin*." Cara adds after some thought, "At least he gave you a plain T-shirt."

"Max gave me the shirt." Reed runs his hands over his torso. "I guess teenagers like the snugger fit."

Cara apologizes profusely. It didn't occur to her that Reed, Carter, and Far Guard would run out of clean clothes. She promises to dig some up for them and run a load of their laundry after breakfast.

"C, we're big boys, we can fend for ourselves. No need to apologize."

Cara smiles knowing he's right, but she is struck by the camaraderie developing within the walls of her home from this divergent group of people. She's jolted out of her thoughts when she receives a flick to the back of her head.

"You like my choice," Sasha says from behind her, making it a statement rather than a question.

Cara should reach back and smack him for the flick, but his choice of jeans for Reed is still resonating in her mind with inspiration and concern. Feelings she's going to have to resolve later when she has more time to process them. Sasha takes the seat at the end of the table with a cup of coffee and gives Cara a little smirk. Then she notices his outfit.

Deciding not to address the jeans choice for Reed, Cara inquires, "And what the hell are you wearing? You look...um...normal."

Sasha has on a long sleeved fitted black shirt with army green cargo pants. No decals, paints, or jewels. His hair is pulled back into a small bun on the back of his head. He looks like a hipster. He's adorable, and younger looking with his hair pulled entirely off his face. He hasn't shaved, adding to the cuteness factor because he's sporting a fuller, trimmed beard. Cara turns to cop a glance at her husband. Nic hasn't shaved, either.

"Nic, Jake and I are going on a weapons mission," Sasha advises, raising one eyebrow.

Cara looks to Jake for some sort of explanation. "We are going to put together everything we have between the three of us, locally, to see if we have enough firepower. Then we'll stockpile it in the garage and start outfitting the vehicles and the house," Jake declares impassively around a mouthful of pancakes.

"We need to make sure we're ready in case something should go down. Reed has offered up some additional weapons if we determine we require more," Jake adds.

Nic serves Cara and Sasha each a plate of pancakes. He leans into his wife. "We need to decide if we're going to send the kids to school tomorrow. Jake and I have discussed it, and we think they should go."

Schools have already become a dangerous place, lately. The high school has excellent lockdown procedures and utilizes the ALICE plan, an acronym for alert, lockdown, inform, counter, and evacuate, but the thought of the kids being away from them all day is frightening. Both Cara and Jinx feel the kids should stay home. Missing some school won't kill them, but going, may. She discussed the topic in depth with Jinx last night.

"Reed's working on something he thinks may make us feel better about letting them go," Jinx sighs out.

Reed explains he's working on getting Carter and two of the FBI Agents inserted as substitute teachers at the high school in the classes the kids have. He hopes to speak directly with the School Superintendent today. Reed just needs to figure out what spin he wants to place on this to protect all of them from speculation.

Nic adds, "Cara, we can't keep them hidden here at the house, indefinitely. We can pull Max from all sports, because I don't like the odds of him exposed in an open field, but at school, with protection, I think we do it."

"I see the logic, I do, but…" Cara can't finish her thought out loud. *As their mother, I can't get the wretched fear for their safety out of my heart.* For the first time since their enlightenment, Cara sends this statement out to all their threads.

Shifting their heads around to one another, they attempt to determine if they did all hear that.

"Nice trick," Reed says when he realizes they have all received the same message.

It's a trick I intend to use often if it keeps us all safe. Cara's response is delivered with a stern reprimand to the group.

Jake asks, "Can anyone communicate back to you, besides Nic?"

Cara looks subtly to Sasha, wondering if he's comfortable with her letting them know. He nods slowly. "Sasha and I can communicate. He can with Nic, too."

Jake's eyebrows shoot up in surprise, but then he thinks for a moment. "I'm not surprised, really. I think we all may be able to perform that at some point." Questioning Sasha, "How did you do it?"

Sasha gives Jake a boyish shrug. "I'm not sure, but I believe it has more to do with trusting than anything else. I figured out where I need to be in my mind to push my thoughts to them. You called it blocking. The natural block must come down on that section of your mind. Because Nic and Cara don't have many blocks to each other, they found the connection easily. I also figured out the energy push. We do convey it preformatted, Jake. I can send whatever emotional energy boost I want. Again, not entirely sure how I am doing it, but I only think of the emotion I want to convey and push it out."

Sasha looks to her with a nod to confirm his statement. Cara adds, "Last night I sent him loving energy at dinner and again during the video.

Later, he sent me something that felt like courage after our discussion with the kids. We can both do it."

Again, Jake's eyebrows rise. "Interesting."

Jake ponders for some time and no one speaks, sensing he is deep in thought. Finally, he advises, "It would be prudent to practice some of that today. As Cara indicated, if we can communicate to each other nonverbally and quickly, the odds in any confrontation are going to rise substantially in our favor."

Nic sits at the table with a plate of pancakes for himself. Cara rises to get more coffee and brings the carafe to everyone for refills. They decide Jinx and Cara will work with Reed and the school administration this morning. Cara has a neighbor who's a teacher at the school. She will be able to provide cell phone numbers for the superintendent and principal.

The boys can work on creating their armory, and then everyone will spend time practicing their gifts on each other.

Nic announces as he eats, "I'm done cooking. Kitchen is closed."

"Carter will be disappointed he missed Mean Man's Mean Breakfast," Cara giggles out as she places the carafe back on the warmer.

CHAPTER 15

THE MORNING GOES WELL. REED spins a yarn to explain why the kids will require additional protection. Carter and the two other agents/substitute teachers will be armed, and at the school, before drop-off for this week. Nic, Sasha and Jake have assembled what looks like a military arsenal in their garage. Reed and the girls wander out to inspect their activity. Cara and Jinx are stunned to learn the boys have this much firepower hanging around.

Jinx, don't tell them, but I'm impressed this has all been local and we never found it. I'm not sure if that's kudos to them, or a hand slap to us.

Sitting on a set up folding table is a stripped down M4 Assault rifle. Jinx approaches it. Jake sees her and warns, "Honey, be careful not to touch that."

Jinx scowls back at her husband before reaching for the pieces and, quickly and effortlessly assembling the rifle. Before he can react, she has it pointed right at him. "What part of be careful are you referring to? The part about shooting your ignorant ass?"

Cara and Reed burst out laughing, almost uncontrollably. Nic and Sasha join them. Jake is still staring at his wife in total disbelief. Jinx lowers the rifle and field strips it once again, all while keeping her narrowed eyes primed on her husband.

Jake draws closer to her and says rather loudly, "You don't know how turned on I am right now." Of course, this elicits a further round of laughter from the group. Bowing his head to Cara and Jinx, he adds, "My apologies, ladies. I haven't wrapped my head around any of your skills, yet. But it must be years since you've handled a weapon."

Cara and Jinx cast a quick glance at each other before Jinx offers, "Not really. Cara and I go to the gun range once a month to practice. We find it...therapeutic."

Nic snaps his head to Cara with this admission. "You do? Wait...but you don't train?" Cara's eyes shift to Reed quickly, and that's all it takes for Nic to sputter, "Oh my God! Your weekends away with Reed!" Shaking his head with derision, he admits, "Here I was picturing you both arm in arm at some Gala, or seeing a show, but it's more than that, isn't it? You've been running ops!"

Cara comes closer to her husband. "No, not ops in that sense. Not. At. All. It's more training. And sometimes I do Reed a favor and attend functions as his date but...with an ulterior motive... to gather intel. It's perfectly safe, and no threat of injury to me."

Nic is scowling at both Cara and Reed.

"I've enjoyed it, like you have. It keeps me sharp without feeling threatened," Cara adds.

Nic processes this new information for a moment. "So, what do you two do when you aren't on an intel gathering mission?"

Reed responds, "We train in the ways we've always trained together. C is my best field partner, and I think we both derive the maximum benefit when we do it together."

"And what exactly is this training?" Nic narrows his eyes at the man.

Reed glances subtly to Jake. "I don't think it's warranted we discuss it. All you need to know is C's still training."

Baby, I'm not sure how I feel about this. On the one hand, I'm very relieved to find out you and your boyfriend aren't spending romantic weekends away together as I envisioned. But on the other hand, now being privy to your team MO, I am not happy about Reed having his hands all over my wife.

Nic, there's none of that. Honestly, we evolved beyond those sex scams, early on. This other training is...unorthodox, and not something I'm prepared to share with the group. I'm not prepared to share it with you either, at least not yet. It's complicated, NOT romantic but a very different approach to training that Reed and I mastered early on in our professional relationship.

I feel your emotions, cara mia. You think I will judge you. More so than last night?

Yes, and to be honest, I would rather show you the training someday versus explain it.

Fair enough. I guess I owe you that after the Jake thing. Her husband ran missions for Jake for years and never confessed to her until days ago.

Cara smiles at her husband. The trust between them is so evident, even with those few mental comments. Cara wanders over to the weapons cache to see if there's anything she isn't familiar with. "No Tasers? I think I need a Taser since I've recently been on the receiving end of one."

Jake looks at her disapprovingly. "I will see what I can do. Reed, you want to help outfit the vehicles?"

Reed reviews the collection with a critical eye. "No, I'm going to help Cara and Jinx with lunch, practice the mind thing, and see if I can get you guys some Stinger portable surface to air missiles this afternoon."

Sasha is impressed and gazes at Reed with new appreciation. "Dude, that would be awesome!" Reed smirks at him as they head back into the house.

After they are out of earshot, Jake turns scornfully to Sasha. "You're liking him now?"

"Maybe." Sasha looks around the garage before continuing, "I do like Reed, much more than I thought I would. I'm beginning to respect him, too, which is unusual for me. You know I have a very short list of people I respect."

Jake looks at both Sasha and Nic with piercing eyes. "You know this person *isn't* Director Connor Reed of Washington, DC, right?"

Nic and Sasha are stunned by this admission, as if Jake is insinuating this Reed is some sort of doppelgänger.

Jake realizes his misuse of words. "Of course, it's Reed. But DC Reed is a ruthless bureaucrat, a master manipulator, and aggressively aloof. He's a scary man. No one likes to go up against him." At the Pentagon, people begin to sweat when they know he's coming to a meeting. Most of the military know Reed's reputation. Not only do they fear him now, but they know all his background stories. Unlike most of his predecessors, Reed was in the field. He came up through the ranks at the CIA. There were no special bureaucratic confirmations. Reed earned that job, and he does it better than anyone before him.

Jake looks at the door he just left through. "I don't know THIS Reed."

Nic nods in understanding. "You believe this Reed is not to be trusted?"

Jake's not comfortable sharing any detailed knowledge he has about Reed. If Nic and Sasha knew the stories firsthand as he does, they would understand his trepidation. Honestly, he is having serious trouble still reconciling Cara is Agent Chase Bennett. He was blown away when he found out. He never saw that coming, let alone that his own wife was her analyst. Jake has respected his wife and Cara over the years for their wit and intelligence but now he's slightly intimidated by all three of them.

He's going to withhold that concern from Nic and Sasha as well. "No, I'm not saying he's not to be trusted but…I'm just…I'm having difficulty reconciling the two Reeds," Jake merely admits.

Nic continues to nod in support and he can't believe what he's about to verbalize, but he knows this is genuine Reed. He doesn't know how to be anything else when he's with Cara. There is no pretense between them. Nic's been around the two of them together, often and long enough to know the real Connor Reed.

Shaking his head at the memories, Nic lets a secret smile form on his lips while thinking about his wife and her ridiculous boyfriend. They were always so funny and entertaining, albeit, disturbing to watch. "DC Reed is the persona he has worked hard to create. Sound familiar?"

"I'm not an idiot, Supermind. I get the correlation you're making to us, but it's different with us. We are ruthless killers on some level, always. That being the case, then on some level Reed is also innately ruthless," Jake retorts.

Nic disagrees. He learned something from his experience with Cara in Berlin. After his rage over his wife running to her boyfriend instead of her own husband, he understood how she could have done that. He is not the Dark Angel when he's with her. He is just Nic. He has never shown her the slightest inclination otherwise, and not because he was trying to conceal it. "I am Nic Andre, businessman, father, and husband. The Zen Master of this household. Not ruthless. Pacifist. No cover. It's who I am."

Jake stares at Nic trying to digest his words. "Are you losing your edge?"

"There are 546 different ways I could kill you in this garage, including 15 ways with my bare hands. And I wouldn't hesitate to do it, if provoked. But that's the difference. Provocation." When he needs to, Nic can be the Dark Angel. That training exists, but it doesn't define him. "If you don't feel that way, I guess I'm sorry for you. I'm certain Sasha shares my sentiment on this."

Jake is mildly distressed by Nic's words. He is rendered speechless.

Nic, trying to infuse some humor, adds, "I believe the girls would say you need to put on your Freud hat and examine your feelings. Maybe you are not what you imagine yourself to be. Then again, maybe you are. Only you can resolve that."

Pausing for a moment, Nic winces, "And I believe my wife and I are now sharing too much with each other, because I'm beginning to sound like a girl."

While the other three are in the kitchen making sandwiches for everyone, they practice trying to connect to Cara. Jinx and Reed can hear her clearly but can't seem to project their thoughts. Cara admits what they are trying to convey is coming across, but it's jumbled and unclear. Like a bad cell phone connection, their words staccato and intermittent sounding.

Lunch is served on paper plates to everyone spread throughout the house and yard. The kids are in the family room with Carter watching something on Netflix. Far Guard is outside with the FBI boys all trying to help Nic, Sasha, and Jake load the vehicles with concealed weapons. Reed utilizes Cara's office for some privacy. He's making phone calls and is on her PC when she enters with a cold drink for him.

"Knock, knock, can I come in my own office?" She calls out before walking right in, affording him no privacy, as is her norm. Cara has her sandwich balanced on top of her drink in her other hand. She gets comfortable in the guest chair facing her desk.

Starting to eat lunch, she watches Reed bang out email after email on her computer. She doesn't try to communicate. He's in the zone. She just wanted to be near him for some reason. She wants to talk to herself, but she needs to check that Nic is not in her head. Cara does some looking around in there and doesn't sense him.

Weird. Does this mean Nic will always know how much I really spend on shoes? I need to learn how to put memories away where he can't find them. I don't mind sharing, but not the shoes. The shoes must stay hidden.

Cara watches Reed some more. She's almost ready to start talking when Reed, with his back turned to her says, "You want to see something cool? Bring your chair over here."

Dragging her chair around the desk, Cara seats herself in front of her monitors right next to him. He begins to click at the keys and the next thing she sees is an aerial view of her neighborhood scanning across both monitors.

"Watch this." Reed slowly zooms in, and the top of their house comes into view. She can see Sasha's G wagon and Jake's Suburban on the street with the two black sedans. Nic's BMW and Cara's Audi are both parked in the driveway. Nic's Ford Truck must be in the garage getting worked on.

"COOL, Spy drone?" Cara asks, her eyes are wide.

"No, can't seem to shake down the Military to get one of those here." They have a lucky satellite position for the next couple of days, though. By the end of the week, Reed will lose this ability with the rotation of the earth. It's always potluck on the surveillance with satellites. "Tell Nic to walk out to the driveway."

Cara and Reed watch the screens as they see Nic appear from the garage and look up.

Now wave, we can see you.

They watch Nic tentatively wave. They see him go back into the garage and he emerges again, dragging Sasha out with him. Sasha is left gazing up at the heavens as Nic disappears.

Cara articulates a countdown. "8,7,6,5,4,3,2, and 1." On one, Nic appears in her office.

"Let me see. Let me see!" Nic calls out, dragging Cara from her chair. "That's so cool. Satellite?"

Realizing Cara is standing, it occurs to Nic he was rude. He pulls her onto one leg to sit. They're all watching the view of Sasha when they see him turn and look up, like he knows where the camera is. Sasha flips them off from the driveway.

"How did he know?" Reed asks laughing.

"I told him where to look," Nic admits. "Can you zoom back out, but slowly?" They begin to see the street. Sasha appears in the office and stands behind Reed and Nic, wedged between them and the desk.

"This is so cool!" Sasha exclaims.

Reed chuckles as he grasps how long these three have been away from all of this. They haven't had the opportunity to have fun with the new technology. It's a different game out there now. Most espionage is done this way, or with Internet and phone tapping. Seems barbaric in hindsight to think they would send agents to 'spy' and gather intel. Nowadays, field missions are reserved for the final action after countless months of technological analysis. And even then, it takes an act of Congress to commence.

Reed patiently explains to Nic how to control the satellite. Nic catches on quickly and takes command, moving the view towards the neighborhood entrance, but slowly, so the lens can stay focused.

While they watch the screen, Reed details some new protocols they utilize with this technology. He has far fewer field operatives than analysts, currently, under his direction at the Agency. Those analysts spend most of their time just watching video feeds of doorways, for instance, noting who comes in and out, and how often. Personally, he would have hated that kind of work. Reed's thankful his role for the last decade has been merely managing these activities, and not actually performing them.

Nic whines, "Baby, I want my own satellite, and I want it now."

Cara pats his head, "There, there, Veruca. I'm sure Reed will let you play with his."

"But I neeeeed one. How can I be Ernst Stavro Blofeld without it?" Nic continues to pretend whine.

Reed leans back in his chair while Nic plays with the controls. He doesn't know who Veruca is, but Blofeld is his personal favorite villain, Leader of SPECTRE, arch nemesis of James Bond. He lets his mind wander through the possibilities.

Cara must sense the emotion from the diabolical fantasy he's constructing and slaps Reed's chest. "I know what you're feeling, Connor Reed, so get that despicable idea out of your head right now," she scolds.

"Come on C, the villains have all the fun," Reed faux whines, trying to mimic Nic.

Sasha catches on. "SPECTRE. I like it," and places his hand on Reed's shoulder. Nic gives him his killer smile.

"OH MY GOD, the three of you! Stop!" Standing from Nic's lap, she narrows her eyes at them. "I will make you a deal. WHEN we get over this threat, you three can do whatever you like, but until then, please curb your rule the world enthusiasm. Now, don't you two have something to do?"

Reed interrupts her. "Actually, I need to go pick up the missiles. You can stay and play if you like." Nic offers to help Reed, but he hesitates for a moment before responding, "Thanks, but I was going to ask Jake to come and maybe drive me."

Cara goes back to narrowing her eyes at him. "Somehow, I think this is clue number one for Jake."

It's Nic who looks long and hard at him before offering, "It's clue number two."

Cara salutes Reed. She turns back to her husband. He is sure she is going to drill him on what was clue number one she may have missed. Too funny these guys haven't put it all together yet concerning Jake's identity. Reed is especially disappointed in Cara. She should have figured it out by now. Really, when she first met Jake. Jinx, as well. Knowing these two women, they only saw big, gruff, hot, bad boy, and didn't bother looking beyond that.

Reed moves past them with a sly smile as he leaves her office. He asks Cara to log him off when they're done playing. "And do something worthwhile while you're farting around and check for threats."

Cara salutes him again.

CHAPTER 16

DINNER IS IN THE OVEN. Four loads of laundry have been done, including Reed's and Carter's. The kids have been pulled from their weekend party mode and are forced to do homework. Jinx is still hacking ex-British Intelligence officials on her laptop in the kitchen. Nic and Sasha have finished tricking out the last vehicle and are in the process of placing weapons throughout the house. Cara is relaxing while doing work emails in her office.

Nic comes in with a Beretta like the one he used in Berlin, but without the scope and silencer. "Where do you want this, baby?"

Cara stops typing and looks at the 9mm semi-automatic. She places her hand out for it. She releases the magazine, inspects it, and checks the springs on the cartridge. "When's the last time this was fired?"

"Recently."

She snaps the magazine back in, makes sure the safety is on, and reaches for a mailing tape dispenser. She pulls out about 18 inches and tapes the gun under her desk above the kneehole space. "Happy?"

Nic leans in close to her and places his lips on her neck. "I think Jake is right. Watching you handle a gun is a big turn on."

"That's because they're phallic. Now get out and let me finish working. Dinner will be served when Jake and Reed return. Go." She manages to grab his butt while he walks away.

Everyone, including the kids, Carter, and Far Guard, is at the table tonight. It's like a traditional Sunday dinner. The mixed company, a mashup of ages and roles, opens the conversation to a myriad of subjects. The topics are interesting and entertaining.

They learn Agent William Carter, or Willy at home, is from New Orleans. He regales everyone with stories of gators, creole traditions and jazz music. New Orleans is one of Cara and Nic's favorite cities in the States, so they add their beloved places to Carter's list. They realize quickly, as the discussion continues, Carter hasn't experienced his hometown on the same kind of budget they have.

When did WE get to be snobs? Cara asks her husband.

We're not snobs…just because we stay at and eat in four- and five-star establishments when we travel?

Um, yeah. That was sort of embarrassing just now. I feel like Carter was one of those little bayou boys fishing for catfish to make a living. Or whatever it is they fish for in the bayou.

THAT sounded snobbish. And there are catfish in the Bayou and bass… and crappie.

Cara smiles at her husband. She's enjoying this telepathy thing, even if it means she needs to come clean about the shoes. She looks around the table, struck again by the fun and camaraderie. Even Jake and Reed seem closer since their little ride together, the details of which they shared with no one.

No, cara mia, they all can't come live with us.

Cara frowns, but she notices Nic looking at Sasha. *They must be talking. Those two. Too cute.*

Heard that. Still connected.

Damn, do you know about the shoes?

What about the shoes?

Nothing. What are you and Sasha talking about?

We're trying to figure out a gameplan for dropping off the kids tomorrow morning.

Can you patch me into your conversation?

Sash? Cara?

Cara giggles, *Ha, you sound like a conference call. Did you have to hit the flash button on your grid?*

You are a wiseass even in my mind, Vizzini.

Captain, what course of action do you intend tomorrow morning?

Appreciating her deference, Sasha states, *That's better. I was thinking you and Reed take the kids to school in the Audi. Jake will drive in with Eli at the same time. Nic and I, with my wagon, will be in the area.*

You guys want back up position?

I think we're more comfortable watching and scanning, yes. Does that work for you?

Sure, but you know I HATE drop-off. Although, it'll be fun to put Reed through it.

It's a plan then. Cara, convey that to Reed. After dinner, I'm going to my room to try the UK again. I still want to reach my associate there. I assume Nic told you about that?

Um, I was in attendance during your conversation. Sorry.

Nicolae, I am disappointed. Are there no secrets anymore?

Chill Broody, we've had enough secrets for the last 17 years. Welcome to the Brave New World.

Welcome, indeed.

Nic finally gets a thought in. *You two are cracking me up. I'm hanging up now.*

Dinner is long, but entertaining. By the time it's done and the kitchen is cleaned, it's 9:00 PM. Jinx, Eli and Jake leave, and the kids head to their rooms. The plan is set for the morning.

Cara heads to her bedroom to get comfy in her yoga pants and a T-shirt. She finds Nic in the bathroom stepping out of the shower. Taking a long look at his body as he towels off, she reaffirms she will never tire of admiring him.

Catching her seductive stare, Nic goads her with, "Reed is leaving tomorrow afternoon."

He must attend some meetings but is going to leave Carter there and be back by Thursday. For some reason, though, Nic doesn't think these three co-conspirators will wait until Thursday to strike. "I feel it's imminent."

"I do, too. Reed feels badly about leaving, but I know he must get back at some point. In an extremely surreal way, this has been sort of fun, you know?"

"Fun?"

Of course, it's not fun because of the looming threat hanging over their heads, but Cara has enjoyed their time together. This group is calming, but energizing and inspirational. Even Carter. His thoughts don't come exploding at her. She needs to dig a bit with him. Not having to deal with all that outside chatter has made her feel more focused, despite the recent chaos. All the energy these others provide, and emit, probably has something to do with that. "Mostly, I've enjoyed the camaraderie we've established."

"You sure it wasn't just fun because you got to be with Reed?"

Cara folds her arms over her chest and glowers at her husband. Nic drops the towel and turns to her, naked, and folds his arms over his chest.

"He's in love with you, cara mia."

"Argh, he THINKS he's in love with me," Cara states firmly, stomping her foot on the tile floor.

"Yeah, yeah, yeah, I heard you hashing it out all day...but what is it you feel? Have you at least figured that out?"

Cara uncrosses her arms and sits on her vanity chair in deep thought. Nic pulls on a pair of gym shorts. They are having a mental confrontation. They have been all day, ever since she saw Reed in those pants and Nic read her thoughts. There is a tension filled silence in the bathroom for several minutes while Nic reprimands her, mentally. Cara adds a few barbs back at him, but he commandeers the mental discussion until finally, she agrees.

A resigned Cara sighs, then speaks softly, "You are right, Nic, I do need to deal with this once and for all."

She gets up to leave the bathroom, but as she passes her husband, he grabs her arm. He concentrates on her face for a long while before commanding, "Yes, you do! The way I want, and the way we agreed earlier, but know one thing...I won't wait for you." Cara nods in understanding and walks out of the bathroom, through the bedroom, and out the door.

She heads up the front stairs towards Reed's room. His door is shut, and she knocks gently. She doesn't wait for a reply, but walks in wordlessly. Reed is sitting in bed wearing only drawstring pajama pants. His legs are out in front of him, and his tablet is on his lap. He has his reading glasses on, and Cara is struck by how attractive he is. Sometimes she forgets.

She closes the door and stands in front of it, steeling her emotions, trying to draw some courage from anywhere. Reed places the tablet on the nightstand and takes his glasses off. He motions to Cara by patting the bed beside him.

She approaches the bed and crawls onto it to sit side by side with him. He reaches out to place a hand on her leg. "Tell me what's wrong, my sweetheart." The request comes off his tongue with hesitation, apprehension and fear. He knows why she's here.

"Geneva. We need to discuss what happened in Geneva."

He motions Cara onto his lap. She complies and sits facing him, their faces less than a foot apart. Reed takes his time processing his thoughts and emotions as he searches her face. Fucking Geneva. The bane of his existence. Geneva changed his life. He's not surprised she finally needs to discuss what happened. He releases his breath and speaks thoughtfully and succinctly.

"You were my girl. From the moment I met you, you were MY GIRL. I always wanted you in my life. Sometimes, I thought you were my life. So many times, and I mean so many times, I just wanted to take things to the next level, but something always prevented me from doing it. At first, it was the cover guilt, but then, later, it was the work thing. I just thought…I just thought, eventually, it would work out. I always thought you were my girl. Then, Geneva."

He never thought it could happen. She wasn't into dating and didn't seem to want a relationship with another guy. Just him. Always, just him. Until Geneva.

Of course now, in hindsight, he can say he felt her emotional pull towards Nic and it's what caused his additional distress but, "You broke my heart that night."

Cara places her hands on his face. He wraps his arms around her waist and continues. "You were a mess in Geneva. Really, you were a mess after Kabul. I knew it. I FELT it. I didn't want to acknowledge it, but on some level, I knew it was all coming to an end. You stopped being my girl the moment you came back from Kabul. A place you never should've been in."

Reed took Cara to Geneva thinking he could teach her a lesson. He believed he could convince her of the foolishness of her fixation on the Dark Angel. But she only got worse. She became obsessed. And then she spotted Nic at the Summit, smiling, in the arms of another woman. Reed saw it on Cara's face, and he felt it in his heart.

"It was devastating for me." Reed lowers his head, unable to look Cara in the face. She begins to run her fingers through his hair as he continues.

"I panicked. I had to get you out of there. I couldn't bear the look on your face."

He was beyond emotional when he physically dragged her back to their hotel room. Then she fell apart on him and did the one thing he had waited 10 years for her to do. He was screaming at her about being immature and naïve to think she could manufacture a relationship with the Dark Angel of Death, like some spy versus spy love affair from a movie plot. Then, in the middle of his tirade, with her in tears, her devastation apparent, she blurts out she wants to move their relationship to a physical one. She begs him to become her lover.

"Why did you make that offer? And why then, C? Why, after you break my heart, did you think I would accept?" Reed looks back up to Cara, beseeching. Her hands are still in his hair and their faces are mere inches from each other.

Cara finally responds, "I have seen you angry enough to scream at me, mad enough to want to hit me, and frustrated with the need to strangle me. I spent a good portion of my career testing your patience. But I had never seen you like you were that night. You scared me."

He drops his head in grief. He was awful to her that night. He called her a huge disappointment. Told her she was acting like a teenage girl with her first crush. Blamed her for blowing their mission, and accused her of not caring. It would have been one thing if Nic had shown her any interest, but he never even looked her way.

Before he can respond to her, she adds, "I started to think everything you said to me was true. I had become unbalanced over some crazy crush on a lethal killer. And then the insanity of the night came into clear focus. You weren't just angry or mad or frustrated with me. You felt betrayed."

The pain. It's like it was yesterday and not 17 years ago. He struggles for air as his head falls to her shoulder. He's having trouble verbalizing as she cradles his head into her neck. She continues to run her hands through his hair. All he can do is whisper, "But why would you choose to ask me for a sexual relationship on that night?"

He can hear her inhale. "I felt I had never been fair to you. I felt I owed you the chance, first. I felt...guilty."

He finally has the strength to lift his head, and he draws closer until his lips are faintly against Cara's. He tells her quietly and softly, "I felt your guilt, and I was damned if my first time with you was because you were harboring that emotion."

So much happened to him in the 24 hours after he left Geneva. He didn't shun her as she suspected he had. Instead, he laid out plans to seduce her properly without the guilt, shame and betrayal of the hotel room. But best laid plans and all...he never got the chance to implement. Nicolae Interruptus came along and swept her off her feet. Telling her the truth now, all these years later, will not make any difference. It will only hurt her. He would never willingly hurt her. His feelings and emotional well-being will be secondary to hers. Always.

Before he can continue to dwell on that long ago time, Cara does the unexpected. She pulls slightly away to look him in the eyes. She tugs his head towards hers and places her lips hard against his. Her kiss turns passionate as she explores his mouth. His hands unconsciously pull her tight to him. His arousal is nestled between her legs. She runs her hands from his hair down to his face while his hands move under her shirt.

He finally breaks the kiss, his hands on her rib cage, his fingertips brushing the bottoms of her breasts. Placing soft kisses to the side of her mouth, he whispers, "I was your White Knight. I guess, I thought it meant I was also your Prince Charming."

Cara can't take it anymore. She pulls him into a tight hug, cradling his head against her neck again. "You ARE my dashing White Knight on his noble steed. You always will be, Connor." No matter which direction her life takes, no matter what man she lays in bed with every night, this man will always be the one who gets the credit. He made her, as much as she made him. "Did I ever tell you about the reasoning behind the name I gave you, the White Knight?" Reed shakes his head while still huddled on her shoulder. Picking his head up by the chin, Cara forces him to look into her eyes, tear-filled and remorseful.

"Do you know the Legend of King Arthur? As the story goes, one of the Knights of the Round Table is named Sir Galahad. He is called the White Knight. Not just because he carries a white shield, but because he was the Knight known for his tremendous gallantry and purity. That's how

I have always seen you. My White Knight...my PURE love." Cara waits for him to process this before continuing.

"I somehow knew our relationship was to be kept pure. Perfect and innocent as if tampering with it could possibly destroy it."

It didn't really come together until she saw the jeans he wore today. The white shields Mia painted on them were symbolic of Galahad. She knew why Sasha gave them to Reed, but it was the other symbols on the jeans that struck her instantly and more profoundly. It was the full circle again. It all began to make sense in her head, the thinking portion and the feeling portion coming together.

She moves her hand from his face to place it over his heart. She leans in to cradle her head against his throat and chest. "I have always thought it sardonic the Deputy Director Knighted me Sir Reflex." She remembers it was the awful day of her simulator debacle at Langley. She had inadvertently plugged her Duran Duran music into the building's main sound system, and it played throughout the complex. "I wasn't aware at that point the Assistant Director knew the code name YOU were going to use. My nickname for you."

Ironic, how they both ended up as Knights.

Then, the jeans. It was when she saw the jeans and noticed the various shields that she identified another connection. "You've heard of Sir Lancelot, right? He is known as the Black Knight. He was highly skilled, very brave, and very noble. But Lancelot had a flaw. He fell in love with the King's wife, Guinevere. Lancelot gave up God, country, King and duty to consummate his love." She glances up to him searching his face for understanding.

"Your Dark Angel is the Black Knight," Reed gets out with some pain in his voice.

"Yes."

"It was going to take an act of eternal sacrifice to win you."

"Maybe...but it's the light and dark metaphor I couldn't escape from this morning. And the metaphor was caught on the Templar symbols on your jeans. The Templars, or the Knights of the Round Table, were on a great quest. The quest for the Holy Grail. Do you know who finds the Grail? Only the purest of hearts can. Sir Galahad finds the Grail in the legend. He's the only one worthy of its treasure and knowledge."

137

He understands the direction she's headed and tries to compose himself. "So, if this analogy of yours is to be followed, you're saying our relationship was always supposed to be kept pure because you think I am on a quest to find some treasure?"

"Metaphorically speaking, yes."

Cara pauses to get more comfortable on his lap. Reed needs to really dig down deep for her and put away the emotions and the hormones. Raising her arm to wrap her hand around his nape, she calmly inquires, "Why didn't you ever just take me?"

She knows he's a very sexual guy, yet he never touched her beyond innocent caresses and kisses. Almost as if he knew he couldn't. They have slept together and cuddled. They have been naked together, often, but it's never sexual. It's always pure.

"Connor, you have talked the talk on occasion, but with thousands of opportunities, you have never tried to go down that road. You must realize how odd that is. Particularly for you, Reed, the man who has always taken what he wants."

Reed is driven. He sets his mind on something and he achieves it. Nothing stands in his way. Yet he did not pursue her sexually. If he wanted her that badly, if he had the passion for her, and if being a couple meant that much to him, he would have taken her. She never gave him any indication he couldn't for the first ten years of their relationship. She even offered it to him in Geneva, and he turned her down flat. He grabbed his bag and walked out of their room, leaving her in Switzerland, alone and reeling.

Taking it a step further, what if he had taken them to the next level? What if she never went to Kabul, and never encountered Nic? What if she always stayed his girl? "What if we did finally make love? Then what?"

Reed is confused by this line of questioning. "You mean would we have gotten married?"

"Yes, what would you have done, Connor?"

He knew what she wanted all along. He knew she wanted out of the government work someday. He knew the agent thing was wearing thin on her. If they got married, what was she supposed to do? Get a career? That works for a while. Would they have had children? She wanted kids. Would her career have been over at that point? And what of Reed's career? Would she have been the supportive wife? Home alone while he traveled, caring for their children like a single mom?

And now, with him in his current capacity, what would her life be like? She would have no career whatsoever. She would have a multitude of expectations placed on her as the wife of the Director. Hosting and attending functions would become her full-time position. Cara Callous, with her chatter filled head, among the glitterati. She would no longer be her own person.

Connor Reed was meant for the life he has now. He is destined to make a difference. He is Galahad on the great quest. This fulfills him. Cara would not have fulfilled him in the capacity of lover and wife, partly because she herself would not have been content in that role.

She believes he would've given up everything to make her happy, but would he have been happy? As compatible as they are to each other, ultimately they never did want the same things from their lives.

Yet, he has spent decades thinking he's in love with her.

"But you're not in love with me. You love me and I love you, but we are not intended for physical love. My thread has always been as your Knight, your comrade in arms. It was in the cards that way. And there's the irony. I am the Knight tasked to provide emotion, love, loyalty and support. I'm to assist you on your own Knight's quest. I am not, and will never be, your actual quest. You're looking for the Grail, Connor, and I believe you'll find it. It is scripted. I see it now."

Cara sends Reed everything she can, the emotion, the thoughts, the logic, everything, including her love. She knows it's too much for him, though. She can tell immediately. But she continues transmitting, sitting still with her head on his chest, hugging him hard while he processes all of it.

When Reed can finally articulate, all he says is, "I think I get it."

Cara gazes back into his eyes again. "I will always feel guilty for not having this conversation with you years ago, but honestly, it never made much sense to me until this morning. Initially, I felt guilty that I somehow held you back from meeting the right girl and falling in love, but it wasn't your fate yet. I can't tell you how I know that, but for some reason I feel this quest thing comes first. It's the rationale explaining our bond. I'm embedded in your world providing the pure love you need on your journey."

Cara leans in to place her forehead against his. "I love you, Connor Reed. I always have and I always will. It's a coveted position I take the great honor in being bestowed. I've always said I have your back, but I can stand by your side when you need me, too." She places a gentle kiss on his lips and makes her way out of the bedroom.

CHAPTER 17

WHEN CARA GETS BACK INTO her bedroom, the lights are all off but her small nightstand light is on. It takes a few seconds for her eyes to adjust to the semi darkness. She looks to Nic's side of the bed, and sees it's empty.

Cara lowers her head and leans against the closed bedroom door behind her. She tries to control her breathing while emptying her mind. The session with Reed had been emotionally draining and she's relieved it's over with. She can't manage to release the metaphor from her mind, though. The sight of those jeans struck her so hard this morning. Its symbolic nature materialized out of nowhere and clues began to populate. It was reminiscent of watching bacteria multiply in her mind. Clues were randomly being pulled from sections and attaching themselves to the image of those painted jeans.

It was enlightening, but frightening. She really does see a script for Reed. He is on a quest, a journey involving these gifts. The last couple of days have brought about a breakthrough on so many levels. Cara can't yet determine why the timing coincides with this threat, but it's all tied together, somehow. The last 72 hours were meant to happen. She is positioned at a pivotal moment for all of them. A moment she's beginning to sense was scripted. All these years, everyone kept their secrets, and not one slip up, by any of them. Then, all the secrets and the gifts get revealed with this threat. There is no such thing as a coincidence.

They have all accomplished a great deal in this short period. But Reed? There is so much more to Connor than the others. She isn't sure how she understands this, but she does. Despite the breakthrough that revealed Cara's gifts, she continues to feel a strong intuition she's unable to tie directly to them. Like with the metaphor, her mind is arbitrarily pulling clues based on nothing but symbols. Neither thoughts nor emotions have anything to do with it.

She isn't even sure how she knows the King Arthur story. Cara can't recall ever reading it. Maybe a couple of Monty Python movies from long ago but that's all she can remember. Yet the clues found their way into her mind. Whatever it is Reed is meant to achieve, she will be by his side when he does. This was in the cards for her from the moment she looked into those fierce baby blue eyes of his from the other side of that campus police interview room table.

Suddenly, Cara is shaken from her thoughts. She hears music streaming into her brain. Realizing she's been leaning against the closed door, she pushes off and stalks towards her bathroom. Opening the door, she spies Nic leaning over his sink spitting out toothpaste.

While she rests on the open door jamb with her arms crossed over her chest, she watches Nic rinse his mouth and stand upright to face her. He is naked and very, very aroused. She flashes him a quick grin. "I thought you weren't going to wait up for me? And I can't believe you're playing New Order's Bizarre Love Triangle in your head right now."

This causes Nic to start gesticulating wildly with his arms. "Are you kidding?! After that bizarre love triangle I was just involved in?! How could the song be any more appropriate?" He grabs her hand and places it on his engorged cock. "I just had some sort of strange, homoerotic experience, and I'm very turned on, and VERY freaked out by it!"

Cara begins to giggle as she releases his manhood and steps to her own sink to brush her teeth. Nic is following behind, just inches from her body. As she starts to brush, he begins to paw at her clothes.

"Cara mia, you have too many clothes on. I need them off."

Cara tries to push him away, but he's successful in getting her yoga pants removed. He struggles to get her T-shirt over her head while she has the toothbrush in her mouth.

He stops and moves his lips to her ear to whisper, "Did you really need to have a full make out session with Reed?"

Cara spits her toothpaste out while giggling, "You felt that? I couldn't get a clear path into his mind. It was all over the place. I needed him to hyperfocus, and the making out worked."

"Yeah, it worked, but you shot me into Reed's brain right at that moment, and I was immediately assaulted by the man's desire for you. I was sort of 'overcome'. Full pun intended."

Cara snorts at the image he's just conjured, then glares at him in the mirror. "You are the man with a plan. You are the man that asked me to implicitly trust you. You are the man I was supposed to covertly sneak into my best friend's mind, despite my protests."

Nic can't deny Reed doesn't have some serious sexual desire for her, but that's all it is. She was correct, there is no passion between them. It's only a hormonal, therapeutic appeal. It's like having a piece of chocolate cake placed in front of you. You eat it because it looks good, even if you're not hungry.

He watches his wife wash her face. She and her boyfriend never ate that slice of cake. They sniffed it, they may have even taken a lick, but they did not consume it. They didn't, because on some level they understood they weren't hungry and the cake was just empty calories. It's the only explanation that makes sense to Nic. As much as he hates to do it, he must give Reed credit. He never took advantage. He watched the cake, he protected it and saved it, but Reed never took a bite.

Cara rinses and moves to use the toilet. Nic is still following on her heels. She peers at him from her position and pointedly reminds him, "You swore to never tell me what you did in Reed's mind. I don't want to know. I need to have plausible deniability. Just promise me you didn't leave any damage."

They had struck a deal earlier, before she entered Reed's bedroom. Nic's plan had been to enter Reed's mind stealthily, facilitated by Cara as she distracted him. After that, Nic was on his own with the promise that he would not hurt Reed, but only assist in getting him past his misunderstood emotions for Cara.

"Store that memory somewhere I can never see it, Nic," she demands.

"It's already gone. Have no fears. I didn't do any damage," Nic swears with his right hand up. He is sure he didn't do any damage, but what he did do was risky.

Cara grins at him while he blocks his thoughts from her. "You look too precious, naked, aroused and pledging your allegiance." She washes

143

her hands and turns to him. Taking her bra off, she offers, "Now, you may have me."

Nic wastes no time. He grabs her hand and leads her to their bed. He sits with his back against the headboard and motions for her to get on his lap. Complying, she lowers herself to take him in as she does.

His head falls gently back to hit the headboard as he sighs, "Much better, thank you. You don't need to do anything, just sit. I needed the connection."

Cara leans in so her body is against his. "I guess we'll never know if your plan was required. I thought my discussion with Reed went well."

"Really? The metaphor that's been running in your head since this morning?" Nic teases while he begins to kiss her jaw.

"You don't like my analogy?"

"I like the Gallant Galahad and the pure love part. That does seem to fit you two. It's accurate for what you feel, emotionally. The Grail concept is intriguing, as well. But me, the Black Knight?"

"Are you not more a Black Knight than a Dark Angel?"

"Yes, I see what you were going for, but you are not Guinevere in your scenario. You're another Knight. And furthermore, in the legend, Galahad is Lancelot's illegitimate son, which is way too weird to insert into the equation."

"You are such a smart ass, Nicolae Maximillian Herrmann Andrychenko Andre, whatever your name is." Cara states this as she wiggles her bottom trying to get him riled up. She adds, "By the way, I never had the heart to tell you, but Nic, N.I.C, is the way women in this country spell the nickname. Men use N.I.C.K."

He pushes her away, but only to place his hands over her breasts. "I was teasing you before, and yes, I did figure out the lack of a K was emasculating." Even the Dark Angel gets some things wrong. "You did a great job trying to get Reed to wrap his head around the emotion. I was struck by a thought though, while I was listening to you after I left Reed's mind."

Cara turns serious. "You have a question?"

"I was wondering… if you and Reed had ended up sleeping together in Geneva, where would that have left me?"

Dropping her head, she mumbles, "I don't think you want to ask that question."

"Why?"

"I think you need to ask a different question," Cara says as she rubs her face lightly against his growing facial hair with interest. "You need to ask yourself first, what would you have done if Reed were in my room in Geneva making love to me? Would you still have followed me and tried to make contact?"

Nic turns thoughtful for a moment before he answers, "I did think you were in a relationship with him. It wouldn't have made a difference. I needed to be with you. I still would've pursued you."

"Okay," Cara says calmly, "then the question you want to ask me is, if Reed and I were in a physical relationship, whether it started in Geneva or earlier, what would I have done when I did meet you?"

She must recognize the pleading look on his face because Cara smiles and lets her lips rest against his as she whispers, "The exact same thing would've happened. Just like all those years ago. No one and nothing will ever change the outcome, my love."

Nic bites her lower lip gently before releasing it to place his lips on hers, showing her what a passionate kiss should feel like. He breaks from the kiss leaving her panting for breath. "Cara, we spent last evening in my mind. Can I try something in your mind tonight?" He delivers this with a wicked gleam in his eyes.

"I'm all yours," she breathes while arching her neck to expose her throat.

While leaving small kisses and bites on her neck, Nic gathers all his raw passion for her. Not his love, or any other emotions, he only brings his need. That fire he has always felt for the gorgeous, intelligent and complex woman he holds in his arms. It's a desire so intense, the overwhelming need to claim her takes him every time they make love. He takes his burning desire and travels into her mind.

When she realizes what he's done, her mouth drops open. His hunger and craving bounce around in her head, like they are trapped inside an isolation tank with no other thoughts or emotions allowed in. *I thought you needed a reminder of what true passion feels like, baby.*

Slowly running her fingertips up his torso, she somehow surrounds his emotions with her own inside her mind. The effect isn't just fast and furious. It's frantic and frenzied and completely erotic as they practically attack one another. Hands and mouths are everywhere. It's out of control pure passion and lust reminiscent of their first time together.

They are lost for what feels like hours, with only their longing to lead them. They're grasping for breath and each other as the hunger slowly fades, and exhaustion takes them.

CHAPTER 18

THE ALARM GOES OFF RIGHT at 6:00 AM. Cara doesn't usually hear Nic's alarm, but today it startles her awake. She finds herself sideways on the bed. Most of the blankets and pillows are on the floor in total disarray. She leans over Nic to shut off the alarm. He's still asleep, lying perpendicular to her. Pulling closer to kiss him, she spots the crusted blood on his lip and on the sheet under his face. Her quick inhale wakes him. He opens his eyes and sees her, his killer smile coming first before his face changes and his brows furrow.

He pushes himself upright quickly to look her over with concern. "Baby, I think we got a little out of control last night. You're covered in beard burn and some bruises."

"Yeah? Here's the funny part. I look better than you. Your lip is cut and bleeding." Then she motions to his torso which has scratches over his chest and neck.

Nic touches his lip and winces. "Holy Shit, but that was awesome and so worth it. You look like the morning after, 17 years ago." He is smiling broadly and proudly. The lip cut oozing more blood.

"Yes, but next time we try that trick, let's give ourselves some heal time after," Cara admonishes him.

He starts getting out of bed, but not before giving her another inspection. Just as he rises, he grabs between his legs. "Even my dick is sore."

This sends Cara into fits of laughter. "Get cleaned up and go make me coffee. I'm jumping in the shower, ALONE. We can't be trusted naked together."

"Agreed," Nic says as he gingerly makes his way to the bathroom.

Cara forgoes the usual morning drop off attire. She pulls her wet hair into a ponytail and heads out for some coffee. She barely makes it into the kitchen before she hears the whistles and catcalls. She stops dead when she sees the three men seated at the table, all wearing big, stupid grins of delight. She keeps her eyes on them while moving slowly toward the coffee maker to pour hot coffee into a mug Nic has left for her.

"What?" She questions as she draws closer to the table.

Reed rises and struts over to her. Taking her in from head to toe, he walks behind her for the same examination. He's still clutching his coffee mug when he releases that long, slow whistle again. "Agent Bennett, I haven't seen you look like this in decades. And no one ever filled out cargos as nicely as you. Are these your lucky ones?"

Cara waits to respond so she can admire Reed's outfit. He has opted out of his usual suit and is also wearing black cargos and a fitted off-white shirt. He's like a photo negative of Cara, who has on her lucky sand-colored cargos with black combat boots and a fitted, high neck, long sleeved black shirt, her cargos a smidge too tight. She isn't entirely the same size she was 20 years ago.

Sasha lets out his own high-pitched whistle. "Cara, you look, I hate to say it, HOT. The beard burn adds a nice touch. We've already harassed your husband over the shot you gave him to the face."

Cara flips him off before asking, "What is it with you guys and girls with guns and combat attire? They're just my mission clothes and yes, Director, sir, these are the one and only lucky cargos."

Reed doesn't respond but gives her a quick pat down. "I see you're armed as usual for this outfit, Agent."

"Yes, sir, standard protocol."

"Good, Agent Bennett, now sit down and have some coffee and breakfast," Reed commands.

Nic is still smiling, the cut on his lip slightly bleeding from the pull. Cara makes the motion for him to dab the blood before adding to Reed, "Sir, I see you've brought your mission clothes."

"Why Agent Bennett, would you have expected less of me?"

Nic starts giggling and her heart warms. Maybe her husband has finally let go of the consuming jealousy over her antics with her boyfriend.

After last night, he's much more relaxed about it. It certainly helps that Reed isn't emitting anything but pride and respect this morning.

Nic points to them. "So formal?"

Cara laughs a little before explaining they really try to be professional in public, especially if anyone of rank is present. Otherwise, she never addressed Reed with any formality.

Sasha is still smiling as if he can't get over the rapport between her and Reed. Then his smile fades a bit. "You ready, Vizzini?"

"Yes, as much as I'll ever be. Are Carter and the FBI in position?"

Carter has checked in. They're registered at the school and in their classrooms. Reed will text him when they leave. Carter will wait for the kids just inside the drop off doorway. Jake has checked in. He'll time his drop off with Eli right behind them.

"Good. We are a go then. Um, I see all three of you are sporting the no-shave, concealing your facial features look," Cara points out.

"It's a proven fact that the disguise works, and anyway, it can't hurt." Sasha comments.

"Well, maybe my beard burn will contribute to my concealment." Cara jokes.

They all finish their breakfast while Nic prepares the requisite lunch sacks and pushes the kids along. They arrive in the kitchen at 7:10 AM. Max is his usual calm, but Mia appears distressed.

"Mom, what the hell are you wearing? Your regular drop off uniform is bad enough, and now this?" Mia hisses, pointing towards her mother.

Before Cara can answer, Reed rises and places a gentle hand on Mia's shoulder. "Your Mom is mission ready. Get used to it."

This causes Mia's eyebrows to rise. She has no retort.

Without thinking much about it, Cara gets up, grabs the two lunch sacks and prepares to walk out to the car.

Nic stops her before she hits the garage door. He pulls her in for a tight hug as he whispers, "Please, be careful."

It's then she realizes this isn't a normal morning but a potentially dangerous mission. She stops and turns to her children who are behind her. She pulls them both in for a group hug with Nic. They resist, but she doesn't care. As she grips them tightly, the strangest sensation comes over her. She takes each child's hand and states firmly, "Promise me you will do exactly as I ask if it should ever come to that. PROMISE ME." Max and Mia nod solemnly. "Good. Let's rock and roll."

Cara drives while Reed takes the shotgun position. Max is behind his mother in the back seat; Mia is right behind Reed. They pull out of the driveway only 30 seconds after Nic and Sasha leave in Sasha's G wagon with Sasha driving. As they leave the neighborhood, Max requests the music from channel 2 on Cara's satellite radio. She knows he likes to listen to music on the ride, so she complies, leaving the volume low. Only the music can be heard while no one communicates. Cara glances at the cup holders. She realizes she forgot her coffee but notices Reed's. She takes his and drinks.

With a frown on his face, he watches her consume most of his coffee while she navigates the car. Except for his dick, nothing of Reed's is off limits to her.

They approach the school turn off and spot Jake in his Suburban on a side street ready to pull behind them. Problem is Cara has two other parents stuck to her ass. Jake must wait for the two cars before he can pull out. They take the final left turn into the school before taking the first right into the oval.

Drop off is more congested than usual. The slight misty rain is most likely contributing to the volume of traffic. As they proceed into the oval at the 6:00 position, Cara looks in her rearview mirror to see Jake is still two cars behind. She looks forward again and slams her brakes. A teenager has darted out right in front of her.

"Jesus Christ, don't they look?" Reed yells.

Mia giggles in the back seat. "Uncle Reed, welcome to my parents' worst nightmare. The Oval."

Cara smiles. "It's true. On most mornings, I could kill everyone in here."

From the back seat both children yell, "NO!"

"What?" Cara asks alarmed.

Max states calmly, "Mom, you can't say stuff like that anymore. Now we know you can kill them. Please don't."

"Your father and I promise not to shoot to kill, just maim, deal?" Cara smiles once more.

They advance with the usual rubber-necking stop and go until they get to the 12:00 position. Cara is scanning all around her and she can see Reed's head in motion, as well. The one-way in moves in a counterclockwise direction. The school building doesn't begin until the 11:00 position and the front doors are at 9:00. *Almost there.*

Cara glances in her mirror again, looking to spot Jake. For some reason, she feels the need to call him via Bluetooth in the car. She quickly uses the controls on her steering column and Jake comes through on the car's speaker.

"What's up? You good?" Jake inquires.

Before Cara can respond, their thoughts hit her like a landslide. She doesn't wait to process, she doesn't bother to speak, she lets her years of training take over. Cara throws the car into reverse, backing up so fast and accurately, she misses the car behind her by a hair. She throws the car back into drive, yanks the wheel hard to the right, hopping the curb and flooring it across the adjacent soccer field.

"JAKE! Incoming from the parking spaces!" Cara yells in her car.

She looks in her mirror to see two cars emerge from the end interior parking spaces of the oval, gunning towards the spot she just vacated.

Nic. Grid. Now! Location of the weapons in the car.

A grid emerges in Cara's mind like a map of the interior of her vehicle. She quickly sends it to Reed, who immediately pulls open the glove box and reaches under his seat. She's still flooring it across the soccer field and can see the two other vehicles following. Simultaneously out loud and in her mind, she yells, "Black Tahoe and black Crown Vic in pursuit. Can't see plates."

Jake responds, "Am bypassing queue to drop off Eli and will be right behind you. Get Carter outside to meet up with me!"

Reed has his phone in hand and is texting. They can hear Jake opening doors in his car and screaming at Carter who's now standing in front of the school with his gun drawn.

"Carter, take him inside and lock down the school, NOW!"

Cara veers right off the soccer field onto the adjacent street and puts the pedal to the metal. She begins to weave around every car on both sides. She reaches quickly behind to her daughter. "Mia, I need paths! I know you can do this. Your father, your brother, Sasha, Reed and me, all together. Make it like a conference call in our minds."

Mia struggles a bit, but within seconds, Cara can feel them all on the same path.

We're heading East on Elm; I want to get away from the school and collateral. Trying for Route 89. It's open and more accessible. Head that way. Again, she says it out loud so Jake can hear her.

Reed is on his knees in the front seat. He is locked and loaded when he begins to pull at Mia. "Mia, switch with me, now." Mia looks terrified but complies getting into the front seat. He tells her to stay down, try to get most of her body into the footwell as low as possible, but put her seatbelt on. He turns to Max. "You too, down as low as the belt can take you. C, they're 100 yards and closing."

60 seconds to the intersection of 89 and Elm, Cara. Sasha's voice is lacking its usual calm.

We are approaching...now. Cara swerves onto State Route 89, avoiding all the cars, and begins weaving through traffic at a much higher rate of speed. She's clocking 85 in a 45, the Audi darting around the stunned vehicles. She glances quickly behind her to see the two vehicles still in pursuit, keeping up but not making as much progress.

"Jake! Where are you in proximity to them?" Cara calls.

"I have them in my sights, but they're 120 yards ahead."

That's when Cara hears it. She turns to see Reed's hands reach out for Max and Mia on instinct. He hears it, too.

"Jake! Incoming rotors!" She sends that out the path as well.

"WHAT THE FUCK!? How did they get air power?!" Jake yells back.

"I need a visual!" Cara commands.

Reed checks the grid map and pulls binoculars out from under the backseat. He starts scanning. "Incoming at 3:00, three armed Apaches, no markings."

"No identification visible?" Cara calls out.

"No. Jake, you need to see this. These guys look familiar to you?" Reed demands.

They can hear Jake over the speakers, "SHIT, SHIT, SHIT, I need to look! Hang on. I'm trying to get to the binoculars without slowing down."

Don't bother. I have them on mine; sending visual to Jake.

"Jake, Nic's sending you the picture."

There's quiet from the speaker as Cara continues her assault on the road, not stopping or slowing. She looks like a Grand Prix racecar driver.

"What the... Reed?" Jake asks.

"YES!"

"This is the blue team," Jake says very calmly with some confusion mixed in. "I'm digging out my other phone."

Reed yells, "If you have a contact for them, I suggest you use it, NOW!"

Cara begins to open the full sunroof on her vehicle knowing Reed is already prepping the Stinger.

Poor Max is gawking at the weapon laid across the backseat of the car. It's a personal portable infrared homing surface to air missile and his Uncle Reed is rapidly throwing a battery-cooling pack into the handguard.

Cara barks out, "They're on approach. Sasha! ETA?"

We have Jake in our sights. I need to plot a course to intercept. Where are you headed? Nic is prepping the Stinger in this vehicle for the second Apache, so have Reed aim for the lead.

I want open spaces. I'm headed for I-480 South. The highway should be less congested this time of the morning.

Reed has the Stinger armed and is hoisting it up on his shoulder as he aims through the roof for the closest Apache. "We only have one missile in this car, C. Let's hope it scares them off."

Nic is requesting direction from Reed on the open mental path. He has never fired an American Stinger and is having some issues arming it. Sasha is driving like a madman, cutting through yards, across low bed streams and a nature preserve. The Mercedes wagon, with the price tag of a small house is performing as advertised as Sasha expertly switches the lockable differentials on the wheels. Cara continues to hear all the mental conversations as she drives like her mother's crush Kimi Raikkonen, the Formula One Ice Man.

The first Apache closes in just as they hear Jake through their speaker talking on his other phone to someone other than one of them. They can only hear Jake's side of the conversation.

"Trickster, it's Bishop! What the hell are you doing up in that Apache? What?...Being paid to hunt down rogue KGB agents and a CIA double agent? Do you realize who you're about to shoot at, you asshole? See the man aiming the Stinger at you? Yeah, that would be the sitting Director of the CIA. You're about to shoot Director Connor Reed if he doesn't blow your stupid ass up first, you fucking moron! STAND DOWN NOW! There are civilian children in the vehicle!"

"Who paid you and gave the intel? British Intelligence?! Did you verify the contact? You've been duped, you asshat! See me? I'm in the gray Suburban about 100 yards back. I'm going to find your ass when you land that copter and kick the shit out of you! ABORT NOW!"

Sasha, Nic, you getting this?

So that was the angle. The one they couldn't figure out. Katherine set the three of them up for collusion. She needed the final confirmation of who the Reflex was to put her plan in motion, a full-on assault. It's diabolically brilliant. Connect a former CIA Agent to two rogue KGB agents and you have the makings of a full-blown international conspiracy. She built a case with British Intelligence, somehow getting them to exclude Reed from the intel. The Brits hired the mercenaries to take them out, not wanting their people on US soil.

Cara is furious. *How can they do this without checking in with the Americans? Tricky bitch is a dead woman walking!*

Katherine has been building a case against them for some time, only needing that final confirmation from Vlad to release her assault. She had been working the angle long enough to get Ed sprung from prison as the fall guy when all was said and done.

She knew about Reed. Katherine was aware of his connection to Ed as the arresting officer. Whatever tall tale she spun for MI6, she managed to throw Reed under the bus so far they would deem it necessary to exclude him from the intel. Reed is either anticipated collateral damage or included in the conspiracy scandal with them.

Nic's the one to finally verbalize where all their thoughts have gone. *Katherine factored Reed into her plan. That's what we were missing the other night. Reed is the connection. She needed the final confirmation of Cara as the Reflex. In order to set the plan in motion and have Ed play the fall guy, she promised to take out the Reflex AND the White Knight as revenge for his capture and arrest so many years earlier. MI6's only possible exposure would then be for the elimination of rogue KGB agents she's proven are alive and kicking, and not long dead. It's perfect.*

As the pieces fall into place, Cara suddenly feels a hand on her shoulder. She knows Reed has heard the conversation on the open path. She can feel both his acknowledgement of the hypothesis and his rage.

"Reed, do not stand down with the Stinger until they do!" she warns. Cara watches the Apache formation about to retreat. Just then, they hear the gunfire. "Shit!" She knows the Tahoe has taken position to take the Audi out in a firefight.

Cara uses one arm to steer and maneuver, while with the other, she reaches behind for Max's shirt. She pulls him forward through the opening between the two front seats. "Max, I need you to drive. Can you do it? Sasha says you're great." Max looks nervous but he nods in affirmation.

He begins to crawl through the opening and positions himself on the armrest between the front seats. Cara instructs him to hold the wheel and put his left foot over the gas pedal. She pushes the seat back and gets him on her lap moving his right foot over the gas pedal. She motions for him to raise his butt as she slips around him and onto the armrest.

"Perfect, honey. Great slip in! Two hands on the wheel and hunch down as low as you can without impeding your visual, seatbelt on. Awesome, job!" Cara says as she sneaks a quick kiss to Max's cheek before reaching over to Mia and squeezing her arm. "I am so proud of you both. Max, keep the pace I had and head to the highway entrance for 480 South. Lay on the horn as you hit any intersections, but don't stop. And follow my command, okay, my man?"

Cara slips off the center console and gets into the back seat. She views the grid map and pulls the automatic rifle from the open trunk and the Glock from her cargos. They're being fired upon, but from a distance too far away to make any accurate hits. The Apache helicopters have retreated, and Reed has placed the missile back down across the backseat. She takes a moment to try and scan the occupants in the vehicles. She relays on all frequencies.

Once the gunfire started, all the traffic in between them quickly pulled off the road. Nothing between targets now. "Tahoe is in the lead position. Simon Joseff is front passenger. There's a driver and two others in the back seat. Crown Vic has Ed for sure, getting one other, but no clear read. Probably Katherine. She's blocking and there's no heavy thread to tap. She has talents." Cara can see that much.

"They're gaining on us." Cara stops to think for a moment. She looks down at the missile and sees the battery pack still engaged. "Jake, I have an idea. Slow down to 30 MPH, on my mark."

Cara tries to lift the Stinger off the seat, but it must weigh over 50 pounds when prepped. Reed is in position by the open window on the passenger side of the car. She motions to him to take the missile. "These are heavier than I remember." She forces a smile while she sends Reed her idea.

"I LIKE IT. You call it, on your mark," Reed confirms as he places the missile back on his shoulder, scooting back down to keep it concealed. He's adjusting the range and placing the targeting on manual.

Cara slides her window down and pulls the seatbelt all the way out. She wraps it around her torso for stability in the event she needs to hang out the window and fire back. "Max, slow down to 30 MPH, 10 MPH AT A TIME! Reed, in position!"

Reed nods. He has the Stinger ready and armed. He places one foot on the backseat floor and one foot on the seat but stays crouched. Cara accesses Nic's grid and calculates the math.

"Jake, adjust your speed now! Steady, Max. Perfect. Reed, ready." Cara watches as the Tahoe gets closer, now within 30 yards. "Reed! Now!" Reed pops his head out the roof, aims and manually fires the Stinger as Cara yells, "MAX, GUN IT NOW! FULL THROTTLE, MY MAN!"

The Stinger missile makes a direct hit on the Tahoe, and as if in slow motion, the Tahoe catapults into the air with full forward motion. It is in flames, somersaulting back over front heading directly towards the Audi. Max gives it all the car has, and it looks like they will barely miss getting hit by the flaming SUV, when it slams onto the road right behind them.

"Four down!" Cara yells for everyone to hear.

She watches as the Crown Vic maneuvers around the flaming wreck and guns it for them. Cara leans out her window with the assault rifle and starts firing on them, hoping to slow them down. Reed takes a duplicate position at the other window. The distance is still too great to have any accuracy. She pulls back in.

"We are half a mile from the start of the shopping district just before the highway entrance ramp. ETA to intersect Route 91 is 60 seconds at current speed," Cara calls out.

Cara, we are on 91 and will intersect with you in 45 seconds. Will take out target if possible, Sasha calls out. He really should stop talking. His emotions are resonating through his mental voice. It's making her angry. Her children can detect fear. This is a no fear zone.

They can hear Jake, "Carter has alerts into the state police. I-480's being closed before our ramp access. Police taking position at the exits and entrances. FBI copter enroute to highway Southbound between exits 191 and 192."

"MOM!"

Cara and Reed spin to see the line of traffic in front of them stopped dead.

"Max, slow down and try to use the sidewalks to get around them. You can do it, my boy," Reed calls to him.

FUCKING GREAT, everyone needs to shop this morning. Nic, we're coming to a standstill!

I see the congestion. Close enough, proceeding on foot to you with sniper rifle.

Just as Max is about to jump the curb, a group of daycare children emerge onto the sidewalk. He slams the brakes so hard, they all jolt forward. Mia is snapped up from the footwell. Reed hits the back of her seat as Cara is twisted by the seatbelt still wrapped around her.

"Seat belts off! Out of the car, now!" Reed yells as he opens his door. He waves the daycare kids off the sidewalk with authority. "Get them back inside!" he barks to the two women with them.

Max and Cara materialize from their side, simultaneously. Cara still has the assault rifle over her shoulder, her right hand at the ready and her Glock in her left. She immediately takes position between the Crown Vic and Max, waiting to send cover fire. There are too many cars, though; all pulling out from plaza entrances between her and the Crown Vic.

Cara is about to tell Max to run to Sasha when she sees it. On the other side of the car, Reed is desperately trying to get Mia out. Her seatbelt having jammed, all it takes is that split second of exposure and…it's slow motion, again.

Reed is bending over to pull Mia out. Just as he frees her from the belt, Cara hears the wiz of the bullet hitting him. It was a lucky shot from the woman hanging slightly out of the window on the passenger side of the Crown Vic.

Cara hesitates just for a moment as panic sets in, but she regains her composure in time to catch Ed aiming and preparing to fire right at Max. Her right-handed weapon is down from the panic. The assault rifle isn't ideal to try for Ed without causing collateral damage, anyway. Her left hand isn't accurate enough with the Glock. She does the only thing she can think of. She hurls herself at Max to knock him over. She makes contact with him just as she feels the bullet rip into her hip. She hits the ground with Max underneath her.

"Are you hit, baby?" she whispers in Max's ear.

"I don't think so," he whispers back, petrified.

Send your father this intel and our position. I am hit. Reed is down. Max, take the gun from my left hand. Safety is off. All you need to do is pull the trigger and keep firing until the magazine is empty. Hold it as steady as you can, but keep it hidden underneath me until I tell you. On my mark, only.

Cara peers beneath the Audi to see a woman's feet step over Reed's body and start dragging Mia away. Cara can't catch her breath. *Max, tell your father Katherine has Mia. She's walking North on 91.*

Nic's soothing words squeeze into her brain. *I can hear you, baby, hang in there. I'm on Mia. Sasha and Jake enroute to you.*

Cara looks up to see Ed approaching them from about ten feet away. She's surprised by his still boyish appearance. He's wearing black-rimmed round glasses and giving her a sideways smirk.

"I was afraid I had killed you first, Cara. What fun would that be if you died before you had a chance to see me kill your son? Now you can watch as the Death Eater spawn dies."

Cara is lying on the ground almost directly over her son. Max's head is still exposed. He has her Glock hidden in his right hand under Cara's body. She's just waiting for Ed to get closer to maximize Max's chances of taking him out.

Ed kicks the assault rifle away from Cara's grasp; the contact sending ripples of pain through her body. He raises his gun and aims right at Max's head. Cara is trying to use what's left of her mental energy to access Nic's grid and calculate the moment she must take the chance and have Max expose the Glock and attempt a shot at Ed. Then Cara hears it, his voice coming through her mind crystal clear.

It takes all her energy, but she scoots up over Max's body to cover his head and his eyes as she watches Ed's head explode. She can feel Ed's thread connection to her snap. And she knows...the 360-degree rotation is complete. She has come full circle. What was her true destiny, 25 years ago to the month, has finally been fulfilled.

Standing with one arm stretched over the top of the Audi is Reed. His 9mm still smoking hot from the shot.

Sasha, Ed down, I have Jake in my visual. Go to Mia, please!

Max is trembling under Cara. Reed reaches them and Cara can see the blood coming from his left shoulder. He gets down on his knees and gently lifts her using only his right arm. He wraps it around her waist and applies pressure to her wound. With what little use he has of his left arm, he pulls Max around and under him to cover his face. He doesn't want him to see what's left of Ed, and he knows what's coming next…the media blitz.

Cara is searching over Reed's shoulder for any visual of Nic and Sasha. Her head is falling backwards from the blood loss. She sees nothing but the people running from their cars. She hears nothing but her daughter screaming in her mind.

"Sweetheart, you need to stay with me, please. Promise you'll stay with me." Reed looks at Cara with pleading eyes before leaning into her son. "Max, it's going to be fine. Are you hurt anywhere?"

Max shakes his head. His eyes are watering and all he can get out with a shaky breath is, "Mia."

"Your Dad will get Mia. He's the best," Reed tells him trying to be reassuring.

Jake hits them from a full out run. Phone in hand, he's on it before he even reaches them. They can hear him yelling, "Two Medevac's, NOW!" He ends the call and kneels next to Cara.

"Five minutes. They're landing in the green. Cara, can I lift you up?" Jake requests, but it comes out a shout.

Cara can't even nod. She lets her eyes wander over to Jake as an answer. Jake collects the weapons quickly and hides them in the Audi. Then he reaches for Cara.

CHAPTER 19

NIC IS SPRINTING AT MAXIMUM speed. His lungs are burning. His long leather coat is concealing the rifle and a multitude of other weapons. In this moment, he's not the steely-eyed cold-faced agent. He's a husband and father. He's operating on emotion, his mind reeling. As he runs across the congested main intersection, he can see the top of the Audi on his right. He can also see the G Wagon cutting off pedestrians and cars as it hits the Town Center Green, tearing up the grass as it flies across it. Mia's screams of terror echo in his mind.

Mia, my beautiful girl, it will be all right. I need you to stop struggling with Katherine. Just go with her and try to stay calm. Daddy is coming for you, I promise.

Sasha, I see them heading past the pharmacy. Katherine has a gun in Mia's back. She will most likely turn right past the pharmacy and take cover between the buildings.

Nic can't seem to run fast enough. He has lost connection to Cara, unsure whether she shut him down out of pain, anguish, or her lack of consciousness. Katherine does indeed take Mia around the corner past the pharmacy, and they're now out of his sight.

Mia is pushed into the alley between the two buildings. Katherine has one arm wrapped tightly around her waist and her other hand holds a gun pressed into her back. Mia has stopped struggling, but her whole body is trembling with fear. Her only open connection is to her father at this point.

She has lost her mother and Max. Eli is too distant to connect. Katherine continues to push her down the alley, but she seems to be getting tired and they're moving slower.

Dad, she's slowing down.

Mia, whatever happens I need you to stay as perfectly still as possible and ignore what you hear, okay? Do not react. Everything will be all right. Just listen for me to instruct you.

Just as Katherine and Mia are more than halfway down the alley, Sasha appears at the other end, facing them on their present course. His face is blank and hard. He's wearing his leather biker jacket. He looks ominous, arms held calmly out to his sides, his hands empty and open, palms back. Katherine sees him and comes to an abrupt halt. Mia can hear her loud sharp intake of breath.

"YOU!" Katherine screams as she tightens her grip on Mia.

Sasha remains motionless, his eyes locked on Katherine. He watches her every move and reaction. Speaking to her very softly, he keeps his voice flat. "Katherine, my love, what have you done?"

"DON'T SAY MY NAME, STEFAN, or is it Alexander, or Sasha!? It should be SATAN! You're an abomination on this earth!" Katherine screams at him.

She is wild eyed. Her face contorted with pain and hysteria. Her hair is gray and disheveled. She resembles a witch from a fairy tale.

Again, Sasha answers her, but very calmly with no inflection. "You were so beautiful, Katherine. So young and innocent…you were… so easy." He pauses and tilts his head, "What happened to you? You look wretched now."

Katherine pulls the gun from Mia's side and aims it at Sasha for just a split second before bringing it back to Mia, but pointing it at her head. "I want to kill you so badly for everything you've done to me, but that's not enough punishment for you. I will kill the girl first, and you will watch and enjoy."

Sasha lets out a snort and laughs, "You mean to torture me by killing the child? Really Katherine, you expect me to care? The girl means nothing to me."

"No, you LOVE her. I SAW it. You LIE!" she screams at him defiantly.

Sasha composes his face again. "I lie? You saw my love for the girl? Katherine, you saw my love for you on my face years ago. Did I not lie about that?" He's completely poised when he delivers each blow.

"YES! You're incapable of love. You're the Devil, pure evil!"

"You are correct. I am evil. I did not love you, and I do not love the girl. I do not love anyone," Sasha delivers with total serenity.

Katherine is trembling with rage. Her eyes are frantic as she looks to Mia, and then back at Sasha. "DO NOT TRY TO CONFUSE ME! The girl dies, then I will kill you…"

Katherine loosens her hold on Mia to get a proper angle for a shot at her head.

MIA, DOWN TO YOUR KNEES, NOW!

Mia obeys her father and just lets her legs give out. She catches a glimpse of him behind her. In a split second, her dad has Katherine's gun arm in one of his hands while the other hand rips at Katherine's jaw, snapping her neck. Not a speck of blood, and the wicked witch is dead.

Nic watches as Katherine's body crumples to the ground. He doesn't hesitate or let his eyes linger. He reaches out and grabs Mia into his arms, fiercely. He pulls her tight against him and cradles her head into his chest letting every emotion he was feeling loose.

Sasha runs to them and tightly wraps his arms around them both. No one speaks. They just hang on to each other.

Sasha finally releases them in an effort to regain his composure. "Nic, I will take care of this. GO."

Nic turns to him and understands, still clinging to Mia. He begins to move them back down the alley towards the Town Green. He can't seem to release his grasp on his daughter. She hasn't spoken since the episode began. Her breathing is shallow and rapid and Nic can feel her trembling beneath his arms, although he's not sure if the trembling is all coming from Mia.

He whispers softly to her, "It's all over, beautiful. You were awesome. Try to breathe slowly. Let's go find Mom and Max."

Nic brings them out to the public sidewalk, loosening his two-arm grip on her, keeping just one arm tightly over her shoulders so they don't appear conspicuous.

Jake is carrying Cara across the street towards the Green. Reed is up and walking on his own behind them, but he has Max concealed beneath his right arm. Forget the pain and start spinning, he thinks to himself.

"Max, listen to me. I'm not sure your mom is conscious enough, but you need to understand how I must spin this." He doesn't want Mia, Nic, Sasha or Jake involved if he can help it. He needs to protect them. He needs to shield them. Cara and Max may be too exposed already, but he's still trying to cover Max's face.

Max acknowledges he understands what his uncle is trying to do and reaches out to his father.

Dad, are you and Mia, okay?

Yes, my man, we are fine and on our way to the Green.

Max relays the good news to Reed. He trusts Sasha will know what to do with Katherine. He needs Nic to keep himself and Mia as concealed as he can on approach. They're the grieving, concerned husband and daughter, but they must try not to be photographed. Cameras are already out. Local news vans are approaching.

"Tell your dad to stay in your head. Listen to my story and follow my lead," Reed barks out to Max, but then holds him closer and runs his right hand through Max's hair, affectionately. "I told you your dad would get Mia. And your mom is going to be fine." Reed isn't convinced about the second part of that, but he's forcing his emotions away to focus on damage control.

When they get to one end of the Green, they notice the local police have cordoned off an area for the first of the two helicopters to land.

Jake slows his approach to coincide with Reed's. "Reed, I am no one."

"I'm already on it, Jake. I sent the info through Max to Nic, as well. Deliver Cara and disappear. Check in with Sasha, he may require assistance," Reed commands.

People are beginning to snap photos with their phones and Reed can hear sirens everywhere. He draws Max's head further into his chest for coverage. He looks over to Jake who places his head down, but over Cara's, as they walk. The local police have created a barricade around Reed and Jake. They are escorting them towards the one landed medical helicopter.

The EMT's are rushing towards them, pulling a stretcher in their hands. Jake gently places Cara on it and she moans. She's growing pale; her breathing is labored.

Reed barks at the medical personnel. "Get her in the chopper now, out of view!" He continues to walk Max to the helicopter door and pushes him into it. "Max, keep your head down until your father gets here."

Reed scans the area and spots Nic approaching. He tells the police to let them through. He is aware and in control despite the blood pouring down his chest from his shoulder injury. Good. He's got this. Glancing around him, and despite his size, Reed has already lost Jake in his visual.

One of the EMTs attempts to look at Reed's gunshot wound but he pushes him away. Reed tries to send Nic his thoughts and emotions, hoping he gets a glimpse. Nic seems to understand and walks directly toward the helicopter with his head down, partially covering Mia. Reed meets him there.

Nic can't help himself; he grabs Reed by his good shoulder and brings him in close for a hug. Reed winces from the motion, but Nic places his mouth to his ear. "I can never thank you enough for what you've done for me and my family."

Grabbing Nic's head so it appears as if they're embracing, Reed keeps it inclined away from any cameras. "I would gladly do it again, my friend. Please take care of her. I need to work this out; come up with an angle to keep the rest of you out of it. I can't risk any of you being exposed."

Katherine will be a very complicated political spin, but ultimately easy to keep Cara out of. Ed, on the other hand, is going to be connected to Cara. Reed will work it as best he can, he promises Nic. "Now go, and I'll speak to you at the hospital later. Tell Sasha to expect a call from me. I may need his...expertise." Reed releases Nic's head and turns his back to him while Nic and Mia get into the helicopter.

They take off immediately so the other helicopter can land. Nic finds Cara being worked on when they enter. She looks bad. They have placed an oxygen mask over her face, but her eyes are partially open, and she's holding Max's hand. Her lucky cargos have been cut off and they're field dressing the wound. One of the EMT's is adjusting an IV drip to her arm when they announce the take-off.

Cara sees her daughter under Nic's arm. The anguish leaves her body and undeniable relief overtakes her face. *You got her.*

It's then Nic can hear his wife and feel her suffering. He tries to conceal it from his face, but the pain and the emotions get the better of him and he begins to cry. He's trying to keep it together for her, but the tears are collecting in his eyes. *Cara mia, failure was not an option. I wouldn't let you down, EVER.*

You were scared?

I was…concerned.

This makes Cara smile slightly. *You can let the death grip you have on Mia go now, Angel. I think you're scaring her more. Can you ask her to hold my other hand and sit by me?*

Nic smiles when he realizes he is still clutching Mia to him. He motions for her to go to her mother, sit in the jumpseat and put her seatbelt on.

Cara looks at her daughter and forces a smile while squeezing her hand. Appearing slightly traumatized, but otherwise fine, Mia squeezes her mother's hand in return. Nic scoots in closer to his wife so he can brush the hair from her face. Affectionately, he takes a few moments to run his fingers through it as they fly through the air.

The look on his wife's face is so serious as she addresses their children. *Agent Max, Agent Mia…you guys were totally awesome in the face of danger. Your handlers are very impressed by the results of your first mission. How are you feeling about your efforts?*

This gets both kids to smile.

I really liked the driving fast part. Max gives a devilish grin.

Mia leans over her mother to flick her brother in the head. *You are such an ass, Max.*

EPILOGUE

"CARA, YOU WERE PRETTY LUCKY, although the irony didn't escape me. The bullet traveled at an angle into your hip towards your uterus. Lucky for you, it was removed five years ago."

Nic continues his update after Cara arrives from the recovery room. The doctors were able to extract the bullet with minimal damage to any other organs or bones. She will be on bed rest for a couple days, and then standard post-surgical recuperation and rehab.

The surgeon believes her existing scar tissue from both the C Section and the hysterectomy assisted in slowing the bullet down. Nic suspects the angle and distance were more the contributing factors. And, it was a .22 caliber.

"They must have given Ed the little gun thinking he was useless with anything larger," Nic adds, sitting next to Cara and holding her hand.

Cara nods, slightly disinterested in her injury, or prognosis, and looks around the room. Her children are seated with bags of fast food in front of them. She cringes when she sees it. Eli is sitting with them eating. Sasha is standing with Jinx on the other side of her bed. Alert, and looking like a mean bodyguard over by the closed hospital room door, is Jake.

Cara tries to find her voice. It comes out hoarse and painful. "First time I've been shot."

"Really?!" Sasha exclaims and starts tugging off his shirt to show her his various scars and explain them in detail. Nic takes his shirt off and shows Cara the scar he received when he was knifed and a bullet he took to the arm. Not to be outdone, Jake has approached the bed with his shirt off, and is beginning to unbutton his pants. Thankfully, Jinx stops him before he can reveal too much.

Cara can only smile at the three shirtless men. She sends a little message to Jinx to get her worked up.

"I know! What the hell is it with you guys and being mostly naked? Cover up already!" Jinx yells at them.

Cara reaches out for Jake's hand. He takes it gently. "We would've been Apache meat if it wasn't for you," she croaks out slowly.

"Little darling, is that your way of thanking me?" Jake teases. Cara nods solemnly. Jake waves her off but leans in closer to her, "Cara, YOU were amazing. I still can't believe it, to be honest. Brilliant."

Sasha adds, "Now I see what all the hoopla was over this Reflex." He smiles wide for her.

Cara tries to wave him off, but she can't bring her arm up high enough, so she gives up.

"Vizzini, you really were impressive. Honestly, you handled it better than anyone. You kept your composure, despite having the kids in the car with you. I felt your steely resolve. You, my dear, have captivated me. You may work for me anytime."

"Speaking of who I work for…or maybe I should rephrase that to who WE work for after today, how's Reed doing?" Cara whispers out.

"The man is a piece of work! He was yapping on the phone and barking out orders while they were wheeling him into surgery. I think Reed might have opted for a local just so he could keep command during it," Sasha says with flair.

Cara narrows her eyes at him and turns to Nic hoping someone will answer her. Nic informs her, "Reed is going to be fine. The bullet went through his shoulder. It caused some tissue, muscle and nerve damage, but all of it they were able to repair. He should make a full recovery but will require some rehab. He had a concussion, though. When Reed was shot, the force of the bullet caused him to whack his head on the side of the car door." Nic teases, "He must have a soft skull."

Cara narrows her eyes at him, too. "You guys aren't fooling me with the disparaging comments. Tell me what he's spinning. Cuz, I know my various Reeds, and he is in spin doctor mode right now."

Sasha turns serious and leans in closer to Cara so he can keep his voice low. "The man has talent, I tell you. Reed spun the Ed angle to make it appear as if Ed was seeking vengeance against him as the original arresting officer in his rape case. He spun Simon as the link between Ed and a former rival from his days as an agent. Collectively, they paid to have the Director of the CIA assassinated. Reed then called MI6 and worked out a deal with them, so they now owe him big time after he thoroughly ripped them a new asshole. He kept them out of the press entirely, though."

Still with a strange admiration in his voice, Sasha announces with some pride, "As for the former rival...well, let's just say Reed owes ME for that one."

"Sasha, you didn't offer yourself..." Cara argues.

"No! But I did offer up one of my adversaries," Sasha adds with a wicked smile. Cara knows she won't find out the name of this adversary. That will forever stay between Reed and Sasha.

"But what of the Katherine angle? How was she able to manipulate MI6 for the assistance? What fable did she weave to get them to believe in a conspiracy that may have included the three of us along with the sitting Director of the CIA?" Cara inquires.

"Reed isn't speaking of it, Reflex. He may tell you at some point, but for now, he's playing those cards close to his chest. I don't blame him. At this moment, the less we know, the better, as the political fallout unfolds." Sasha cocks that one brow at her.

Nic interrupts to add, "Reed was able to keep all of us but you and Max out of the equation. Kids and parents at school saw Max in the backseat of the car with Reed at drop off. Because of Mia's position in the car and the angle, she was hidden from view. No one has come forward to report they saw her being dragged away from the Audi by Katherine, so Reed is taking the chance that no one will. Mia was kept home from school today for illness as far as the story goes."

Cara nods in understanding but asks, "And Max and me?"

"Reed is keeping close to the truth there, too many witnesses. And the press will eventually link Ed to you. Reed made a statement admitting you and he have been very close friends since he saved you from Ed's rape attempt 25 years ago. It just happened that he was here visiting you when it all went down. Reed has also manipulated his public calendar so it appears the trip had been planned for months in the event someone checks his story."

There are enough photos of Cara with Reed at various events and galas over the years for the press to verify the tight friendship. Nic adds, "As for Max, there are already pictures making the rounds that show you throwing yourself in front of our son. Fortunately, none of the angles show your weapons yet. There are also pictures of Reed shooting Ed while he was all bloodied up from his own gunshot wound. The press is having a field day with it. The man who was the target of an assassination plot saves his good friend and her son." Nic shakes his head slightly amused.

"I told you, master manipulator. He always knows how to spin it to his advantage. In this day and age of optics, you have to respect that." Cara says it as a statement, denoting nothing but reverence.

"There's even a great grieving shot of the pathetic husband embracing Reed in thanks," Sasha laughs out.

Cara looks to Nic, expecting him to jump over the bed at Sasha, but instead Nic appears thoughtful. He says nothing, but Jake chimes in. "The man had every angle worked out by the time he boarded the medevac. DC Reed is an animal."

"No, Jake, DC Reed is about loyalty and honor. You prove to him you trust him, and he WILL trust you, always. But you must trust him first. You must take the leap of faith first," Cara says thoughtfully.

Is this the Holy Grail thing again? Nic inquires with some mirth.

"Only he with the purest of hearts," Cara utters softly, in deep thought, and then adds, "Maybe with a little help from some Merlin magic."

He saved yours and Max's lives, cara mia. There is no spin we can put on that.

I'm glad you finally understand why he's my best friend. He is and always will be my White Knight. He's always protected me, Nic. And he knew you trusted him to protect the rest of our group from exposure. So, he did it. He isn't a complicated man. He always had a deep respect for you and Sasha, but now that he has your trust, he will be your greatest ally. I can promise you that.

Nic seems to think this over for a while as he and Cara ignore the rest of the conversations.

I was going to take the kids home and come back and spend the night with you here.

You know, as lovely as that sounds, I'm exhausted and crave some serious morphine and some sleep. Besides, I'm worried about the kids and what this ordeal has done to them. I think they need a parent tonight.

169

I get it. I'll be back in the morning after DROP OFF HELL, which subsequently, following this morning, has a whole new meaning... Cara tries for a wide grin and squeezes his hand.

Slowly bringing her hand up to brush kisses to her fingertips, he adds, *I'll give the kids the low down on what to say and what not to reveal at school. They have comprehended some of it already. Reed is supposed to call Sasha later to give him the details of the story he wants the kids to have. He and Sasha believe the kids should go to school tomorrow. The longer they wait to confront this ordeal, the harder it will be. I agree with them.*

Mentally sighing out Nic adds, *Funny about Sasha and Reed...they seem to be really bonding.*

Nic starts to gather up the crew to prepare for their departure. He makes sure to have a nurse administer more pain relief for Cara. Before he goes, he sits alone with her, placing kisses on her face and running his hands through her hair.

"I love you, baby. See you in the morning. I left your cell phone on the nightstand. I called your family and told them you'll be fine. Your mother had the nerve to say how proud she was of Reed for saving you guys." He gives her a wink.

Cara can barely keep her eyes open, but she pulls him to her. "I love you, Lancelot. Are you sure Guinevere doesn't do any fighting in the legend?"

"Now you're just talking rubbish, my fair lady."

"Kiss me one more time, please, brave Sir."

Cara falls into a deep sleep. She dreams of Knights and fair maidens, goblets filled with wine, and shiny ornate chalices. She dreams of great battles on the fields of England, and boundless lovemaking in the castles. She is woken up twice for a vitals check, and on the second visit, she's given more morphine and her catheter is removed.

Each time, she falls back to sleep immediately. She dreams of Nic, his hands through her hair, gently fingering the loose curls and waves; his lips on her neck, softly trailing kisses leading up to her ear with a nibble. The excitement begins coursing through her blood. Nic can always do that to her. His touch is chemical for her. The feeling has never really subsided, even after all these years.

The lips begin to make their way to her jaw, soft kisses trailing his teeth like little, indulgent bites. *Such a turn on.* Her pulse is accelerating and she's getting warm. The lips come so close to hers, just brushing across, teasing for more. When Cara tries to capture them, they're gone and onto her jaw line, trailing again to the other side of her face and onto her neck.

Slowly, the kisses and teeth are making their way to her shoulder, ever so sensually. Her breathing quickens and she's getting even warmer. The lips begin to assault her collarbone, then advance lower until they're just over her breast.

Cara's filled with anticipation; she arches her back as invitation. Those amazing lips move and that tongue licks until he reaches her nipple, the teeth lightly grazing it. She can feel the hand now; the brush of fingertips climbing up her leg, over her hip, across her rib cage, until they meet her other nipple with the slightest touch. Cara is losing herself and lets out a soft moan. Those expert hands and mouth causing havoc. *Best dream, ever.*

His mouth moves leisurely down her rib cage but stops to leave a light kiss across the bandage from her injury. The lips are making their way to her one bare hip, licking, kissing, and scraping. Cara groans her appreciation. The lips are now poised just above her hot spot. She is trembling with need. But the lips pause.

You are so wet for me, my sweetheart.

Cara's eyes open with an audible snap just in time to see Reed take a long, hard lick. She is dazed from the shock of hearing him in her mind, and of relishing the contact, but mostly from the jolt upon realizing he is literally present in her room.

You know how long I've waited to see what you taste like? You taste wonderful.

He takes another lick leaving his lips on longer. Cara shudders slightly from the stimulation of it. She can see him smile up at her with a wicked grin. His mouth moves slowly back to her bare hip with those little kissing lips and scraping teeth. Cara is immobilized. She can't process what's happening. She hears what she thinks is her heart monitor beeping wildly. Maybe that isn't the monitor at all. Maybe it's just her own heart beating out of her chest. His mouth returns to her bandage.

If you weren't injured, I promise you this would be a very long, very pleasurable drive that's VERY MUCH overdue.

Those lips are back, placing soft kisses over her breast before making their way to her neck and onto her chin. His teeth scrape until they're at her mouth. He takes a small bite, pulling her lower lip.

I hate it when you bite your lip because it's always turned me on. All the better when I bite it for you, don't you think?

Reed stops to brush his lips across hers, and then pulls away to look her in the eyes. He grabs her chin with a little force. "I know what you and your Dark Angel did to me last night. Tell your husband he made a slight error. He accidently left a tracer behind in my mind after his intrusion."

If it is even possible, Cara's eyes grow bigger staring back into Reed's.

He lifts one brow and cautions her, "I don't know if I should kill you or thank you. On the one hand, you two had no business being in my mind. How dare you fuck inside my head. On the other hand... *Look and see what new tricks I can do.*

He rises and backs away slowly, continuing to stare into her eyes. Reed grabs her hand and places it firmly over the arousal stretching out his pants. Closing his eyes, he tilts his head back.

I am certain I've never been this hard, my sweetheart. PURE LOVE, MY ASS.

After rubbing it back and forth a couple of times, he gently moves her hand back onto the side of the bed. He places her gown over her and pulls the covers up. Keeping his eyes on hers, he begins to step away from the bed. Cara is still too horrified to move or speak, but she notices he's in a full suit, his left arm in a sling.

"I'm leaving for Washington, shortly. I've checked in with your doctors and you're in good hands." Reed turns to head for the door, but before he reaches it, he flips his head back to her. "You, Nic and Sasha owe me, and I mean to collect, my sweetheart. I'll keep in touch."

And with that, he leaves.

ANOTHER EPILOGUE

HAVING JUST BEEN RELEASED FROM the hospital yesterday, Cara is resting in bed. It's been five days since the altercation with Ed and Katherine, and five days since the incident with Reed. She hasn't heard from him, at all. No calls or texts.

Oddly, her husband hasn't said a word to her either. Nic either has no knowledge of what transpired, or he doesn't want to share. Conversely, Cara has not asked Nic what he did when he was in Reed's mind. The three of them are at a stalemate.

The only person who is speaking, incessantly, with Reed is Sasha. Cara has been getting her updates from him. Apparently, Reed is still healing from his surgery and will undergo physical therapy starting in a few days.

Reed has spun his web, though. No one came forward to say they saw Mia in the car. There are only pictures of her with her father boarding the helicopter. No one saw Jake or Sasha, so they are still ghosts. Reed did admit he and Cara were close friends and he was in town visiting her family. But nothing has come out about her former position. She is only Cara Bianco Andre, Reed's dear friend for years since he saved her from Ed Grotto when she was a young college student. Heartwarming, really. The Press is eating it up. Reed is once again the White Knight, so dashing and everyone's hero. The optics are incredible. His popularity is skyrocketing.

Max is being coached for the media. Unfortunately, there are many pictures of Cara throwing herself in front of her son. And many pictures of Reed killing Ed and saving the both of them. It is being circulated around that Cara will not be able to give interviews because of her gunshot wound. It was serious, and although not life threatening, she is still traumatized by the altercation. Cara Andre is suffering emotionally, and will not be expected to face the Press.

Reed is still protecting her. She will give him that much, for now. What comes down the line later, is still very concerning.

She is broken out of her reverie when both of her children barge into her room in tears. In an automatic response, she bolts up from her lain position. Pain shoots through her lower abdominal area. She flinches and Max knows enough to throw some pillows behind her back.

"What happened? Why are you both crying?"

Sitting next to her, Max gets comfortable with one arm around her. "I don't think I can talk to the Press, Mom." He wipes some tears on her t-shirt. "I mean, I froze. I didn't know what to do and I got you shot. I could have gotten you killed."

Wondering when this revelation was eventually going to hit her children, Cara is not shocked by the admission. Up until Berlin, Cara was in her own deluded Land of Denial. How could she possibly think the progeny of The Reflex and the Dark Angel of Death would never be targets? And now, she is an idiot if she lets herself believe her children will have "normal" lives. Between their gifts and who their parents are, that is not happening for them. And it breaks her heart.

"Max, my beautiful boy, first off, none of us expected you or Mia to handle that situation even half as well as you did. We are very impressed with how you both did manage." Cara pulls him closer to her. "You are experiencing post-traumatic stress. The shock has finally worn off. But we were expecting this. THIS is why Sasha wants to train you both. We want to replace the shock and PTSD with empowerment."

Mia throws herself on the bed, weeping dramatically. "Mom, the Audi seatbelt wasn't stuck." Her tears are coming down harder. "My hands were shaking so badly I couldn't unfasten the belt. Uncle Reed bent inside the car to unhitch me, and he was shot because of it." Her head now on Cara's leg, Mia wails, "I almost got Uncle Reed killed!"

Stroking her daughter's hair and Max's arm, Cara responds, "Guys, I reiterate, neither of you got anyone almost killed. Ed and Katherine almost killed us, not you. Reed and I were hurt protecting both of you." Cara takes in a big breath. "I am your mom, and as such, I will throw myself in front of anyone trying to harm you. What you do or don't do will not make a difference. Both your Uncles Reed and Sasha put themselves in harm's way to protect you, as well. And they will do it again and again."

Her assurances don't appear to placate her children. Cara tries a different tactic. "Besides, from here on in, you will be trained. Maybe... hopefully... you will never need the training. But also maybe, one day you will return the favor and save your old, decrepit mother from near death."

Both her children look into her eyes. "Is that so difficult to believe? Yes, we saved your annoying little butts. One day, you can return the favor. You aren't going to be almost 16 forever. You will mature and grow stronger. You will be better prepared for these situations, assuming that's what you want."

They both nod passionately before Max adds, "But what if I break down during the interviews? I will look like a pussy."

Trying to hide her smile, Cara addresses him. "Max, women love men who can exhibit their vulnerabilities. It's a serious turn on."

He backs away from her to ask, "Really?'

"Of course. You saw your dad cry in the helicopter on the way to the hospital. Did you think he was a pussy?"

Max vehemently shakes his head. "No way! You, Dad, Reed, and Sasha are bad asses!"

"My point, exactly. Be yourself for the interviews. Keep to the script you are given but allow your emotions through. Don't hold them back. The media wants to see authenticity. It will make the story more believable and relatable. That's what your Uncle Reed wants from you."

Finally getting it, Max utters, "Huh."

Mia pipes in with the obvious, "Uncle Reed is counting on Max to appear traumatized and shaken from the whole incident. That's his hook, what he is going to capitalize on."

Hugging both, Cara wipes their eyes before saying, "You have already learned lesson number one. The Press can be your ally. Mainstream and social media are powerful tools you can work to your advantage. Never underestimate what you can achieve with a good spin on any story."

Mia stares pointedly at her. "But if that's the case, why are you not in front of the cameras?"

That is a bit too complicated for her children. She adopts a more obvious scenario. "We don't need for more people to recognize The Reflex.

Agent Chase Bennett is long gone. And that's where she needs to stay."
For now.

They both cuddle into her, and if the world wasn't completely changing around her, holding them close and safe is where she would keep them. Her reality has cracked. The illusion is gone. Nothing is the same. Safety for her children means preparation, training, and vigilance. Even then, there are no guarantees. It's best she adapts to the new normal...and quickly.

AUTHOR'S NOTE

I HOPE YOU ENJOYED THE conclusion to The Reflex. Coming next is The Reaction Part 1. The third book in The Reflex Series.

Find out how Katherine managed to get assistance from the British Government. Just how big and far reaching was this plot to kill Cara, Reed, Max, and Mia? And are they the only targets?

Will training the twins prove beneficial? How will they adapt?

And what of Cara and Reed's relationship? Has she finally gone too far with him? Has she snapped his last nerve? She isn't even sure what Nic did in Reed's mind. How does she attempt to repair this? After being violated, why does she even feel the need to try and repair it?

What about Sasha? Will he finally be able to put what he did to Katherine behind him? Is he ready to move on from all the guilt and anguish? If so, how will he move on?

All these questions and more will be answered in The Reaction Part 1, coming soon.

Check out my page at www.mariadenison.com for updates and info. Leave your email address for my newsletter.

The Reflex Series Spotify playlist is on the website. Like my character Nic, music is important to my life. Unlike my character, I have no musical talent whatsoever. For me, it only makes me appreciate how much talent goes into writing and making music. So, a bow and thanks to all of you devoting your life to the arts.

Thank you so much for all your support.

IN THANKS

I WANTED TO MENTION SOME of the folks who I could not have written these books without. As always, thanks to my family for pizza night when I did not have time to cook. And thank you Uber Eats, Doordash, and Postmates.

Thanks to Traci, Jan, Beth, Vera, Heidi, Lisa, Kaileigh, and Marion for all your test readings and emotional support. Your input was invaluable. Your love, even more so.

Thank you so much to my cover designer (and best sister ever) Claudia Kemmerer!

Thank you to my new copy editor, Kathy Denison, who graciously offered up her services to my much-needed manuscript. Your edits are the bomb!

Finally, thanks to you readers. Please leave positive reviews if you enjoyed the books. If you didn't, sorry, but keep your thoughts to yourself. Just kidding. I have my big girl panties on. Let it rip.

Printed in the United States
by Baker & Taylor Publisher Services